FINAL
NOTICE

FINAL NOTICE

Jonathan Valin

DODD, MEAD & COMPANY
NEW YORK

1 2 3 4 5 6 7 8 9 10

Library of Congress Cataloging in Publication Data

Valin, Jonathan.
  Final Notice.

    I. Title.
PZ4.V158Fi   [PS3572.A4125]   813'.54   80–16654
ISBN 0–396–07898–2

TO KATHERINE

FINAL
NOTICE

1

It was a brand new building, modern-looking in the style of contemporary day schools and community colleges—all glossy undulations and shining declivities, like a razor haircut in concrete and glass. But the old women behind the service desk hadn't changed a bit since the days when suburban libraries were just plaster walls, wood shelving, and "Quiet" signs. They were still little old ladies in floral print dresses and high-topped shoes, wearing too much lipstick or none at all. Wispy grayheads meant to lean together and gossip. Which is what two of them did when they saw me stride through the glass doors—all six feet, three inches of me—with my busted statue's face gone civil in a smile. I

1

figured that they knew every man, woman, and child in the neighborhood by sight. And not only by sight. By record and by reputation, too. By fines and by finitudes. Which, in itself, was probably enough to put the lemons in their looks. That and the fact that they didn't know me.

I asked one of them if she could show me to Leon Ringold's office, and she gave me her overdue frown and looked up coolly from behind rimless spectacles. She was a very little old lady, this one, with round stooped shoulders made for the red cardigan sweater she was wearing and the sharp, chinless head of a night owl.

"I'll see," she said, lingering over the "see" as if being shown to Leon Ringold's office were no sure thing. Then she asked me what she'd been wanting to ask since she and her cronies had seen me come through the door. She did it with a little sweetness in her voice, deliciously, as if she were sucking on a mint.

"May I say who's calling?"

"Harry Stoner," I said. "He's expecting me."

She toddled off to a door behind the desk and walked through it into what appeared to be a small, white-walled office. There was a two or three minute space, which the other old ladies pretended to fill by stamping overdue books and sorting through catalogue cards. Then the owl-eyed one came out the door and back to the desk. She looked, I thought, slightly disappointed. They all looked slightly disappointed. I began to wonder if they didn't know who I was, after all.

"You can go in," she said without enthusiasm.

I went in.

It was indeed a small office, bare except for a steel desk set opposite the door. Leon Ringold, or the man I took to be Leon Ringold, was standing behind that desk; and be-

2

hind him, on the far wall, a muscular wooden Jesus was peering sadly over his shoulder. Ringold was a small man in his late thirties, with wavy, lead-colored hair and an incongruous little boy's face that made him look as swart and peevish as an elf. He held out his right hand as if it hurt him to move; and when I shook it, he swayed slightly at the shoulders.

"Your ladies don't seem to like my looks," I said, sitting across from him at the desk.

He made an exasperated face and said, "Ignore them. They don't want to see Ms. Davis lose her job, that's all. My God, I can't do anything around here without their butting in. It's just like living at home."

I smiled and Ringold blushed from forehead to chin. He had all the makings of a "tetchy" one, as my grandmother used to say. One of those angry little men who've never forgiven the rest of the world for looking down on them, as if a man's stature were purely a matter of height. It didn't take a detective to conclude that the best approach with Mr. Leon Ringold was to stick strictly to business and to save the banter for a client with a thicker hide.

"Ms. Davis is the lady you hired to recover the books?" I said in my best detective's manner.

He nodded and looked deeply moved. "It's unbelievable, isn't it, that a public library would be forced to hire a security guard? But book theft has become a regular epidemic in this country. Why the Hamilton County Library system has lost over a million dollars worth of property in the last three years alone. And do you know why?" He didn't wait for an answer. "I'll tell you why!" he said angrily.

I leaned back in the chair and put on a polite face while Ringold gave me a civics lesson. When he came back to the part about hiring Ms. Davis, I tuned in again.

3

". . . so the Board of Directors hired her to trace books down and to keep an eye on the stacks. Replacement costs are so high that they felt the expense was justified, although I wish I'd been consulted on the choice." Ringold blushed again and I didn't smile. "I'll be honest with you, Stoner. Kate is a liberated young woman whose lifestyle does not suit our conservative clientele. It was a mistake to hire her for this branch. I think the Board can see that, now. She constantly exceeds her authority and has already caused any number of embarrassing incidents. And of course, I'm powerless to intervene."

"You could fire her."

He looked at me as if that was the stupidest thing he'd heard in seven years. "And have them all quit on me?"

"The ladies?"

"Every last one of them," he said grimly. "Ms. Davis keeps them in coffee and in small talk. And they've taken her under their wings. She's one of them." Ringold looked at his office door with disgust.

It was going to be hard to keep from smiling around Leon Ringold.

"For the salary they're paying her, we could have computerized our desk," he said and his little boy's face grew wistful. "You know Honeywell has a dandy two-disc mini, and it doesn't even require a dedicated line. Just a Mode-M and three terminals equipped with Ruby Wands. The darn thing inventories, fines, checks out. All by itself! Gee . . ." He broke out of his trance with a start. "Well, it's too late for that. I'm stuck with the old ladies and Ms. Davis. I don't suppose it would be all that bad if it weren't for this Ripper thing. That's what they're calling it downtown, you know. The Ripper case! What I mean to say is that a number of important people are getting upset. Kate's had college

4

training in criminology and in social work. But this . . ."

Ringold pointed to a folio sitting on the corner of his desk. "Well, take a look for yourself," he said.

It was an Abrams art book. Seventy-five bucks for six dozen handsome photographs and a few meager paragraphs of text. This particular volume was a collection of cinquecento art. Bramante, DaVinci. I skimmed through it, while Ringold whispered, "You see? You see what I mean?"

I saw, all right. Perhaps a little more than Ringold himself saw. Because this wasn't the work of a high school prankster, scribbling scars on the Mona Lisa's forehead like the crosshatching on a road map. No, some puny soul had taken his time, with an Exacto knife and a ruler, and meticulously cut away the genitals, the breasts, the mouths and the eyes of all the delicate looking Italian ladies in the book. Cut them away with a fanatic precision, as if he were carefully excising every source and brand of sexual appeal. Those missing mouths and eyes shook me a little bit. And after a decade or so in this business, I'm not easily shaken.

"How many more of these books are we talking about?" I asked Ringold.

"Over two dozen. About three thousand dollars worth."

I let out a low whistle and he nodded.

"It appears that a majority of them were mutilated in the library itself. Perhaps over a period of months. The art collection is housed on the second floor in a relatively isolated spot. It wouldn't have been difficult for the perpetrator to hide himself away, in the lavatory or in one of the typing carrels. Before we hired Ms. Davis in July, the desk librarian on the second floor was the only supervisor, and she generally had her hands full with the juvies. I do have a list of patrons, some thirty names, who have withdrawn

5

art books over the past two years. You may check them out if you see fit, but my own feeling is that this is the work of an outsider and not a library member. We are a relatively large branch, Stoner. But our budget for purchases and replacements is shockingly small. This," he said, pointing to the folio on his desk, "has got to stop. We simply can't afford to post a permanent guard in front of one shelf of books. Especially a guard with as little experience as Ms. Davis."

He lowered his eyes to indicate just how much was involved. And for some reason that look set off something like a warning bell in my head.

"Why did the Board hire a novice like Ms. Davis in the first place?" I asked him.

"Affirmative action," he said, the way some people say "forced busing." "To tell the truth, she's the protegé of Roscoe Joffrey, my immediate superior."

The warning bell stopped ringing and I looked at Ringold with fresh interest.

"Who's hiring me, Mr. Ringold? Who's paying my salary?"

He sat back slowly in his chair and covered his mouth with his right hand. "I am," he said.

"I see."

"You needn't worry about the money. I have it. I mean, within reason, I have the funds."

I didn't say anything. Despite his boyish looks, Leon Ringold was shaping up as a clever operator. If I nailed his vandal for him, Joffrey's protegé would be discredited and Leon would get his two-disc mini and, maybe, a job downtown. I guess I didn't hold his ambition against him, although I resented the fact that he didn't want me to know what he was up to. Which is a queer kind of vanity for a

6

private detective, Harry, I said to myself.

"Well?" Ringold said impatiently. "Do we have a deal?"

"I'll want to talk to Ms. Davis first. To find out how much work she's already done."

Ringold squirmed in his chair. "You don't seem to understand. I want this investigation handled discreetly. Tact, Stoner. That's what's needed here."

"Tact meaning Ms. Davis isn't supposed to know I'm on the job?"

"That's the general idea, yes."

"I don't do industrial espionage, Mr. Ringold," I said coolly.

He tapped himself on the cheek with a forefinger and looked aghast. "Espionage? I simply want this matter handled confidentially." He tapped his cheek again, rubbed his chin, coughed politely, stared at the markings on a number two pencil, and said: "Well, I don't suppose there would be any harm in consulting with the girl. But, remember, Stoner, this was *your* idea."

2

SHE WAS sitting on a tall wooden stool beside the art collection, reading a worn paperback copy of *The Women's Room*. From where I was standing in the stairwell, she looked very young and a bit studious in her round turtle-shell glasses. Quite pretty, nevertheless. Round, milk-white face. Small nose. Blue eyes. Her blonde hair cut short and set in a tangle of curls that glowed like a cluster of Malaga grapes on a white china plate. I stared at her for a moment before climbing the last stair to the second floor. The way she was perched there, out in the open, she certainly wasn't going to surprise anyone. At least, not anyone with half a brain in his head. And then I wondered just what the hell she planned to do if she did manage to catch Hyde Park's version of Jack the Ripper. She didn't have the big, sinewy muscles you sometimes see on beach girls and on lady jocks, although her shoulders were firm and square and her legs plenty long. Nice legs. What promised to be a nice figure, too.

I walked up to where she was sitting and told her who I was, and she wrinkled her pretty nose as if she'd read something unpleasant in her book.

"Could I talk to you for a few minutes, Ms. Davis?"

She put the book down, slapped her hands on top of it, as if it were a jack-in-the-box with a broken catch, and said, "What do you want?" in a husky voice.

I saw at once that she knew exactly what I wanted, that one of those little old ladies had told her why I was there. I went ahead with the charade anyway, explaining politely that I was a private detective hired by Leon Ringold to act as a security consultant to the library.

That seemed to amuse her, the security consultant part. She plucked off her glasses and said, "Security consultant? Is that the new word for spy?"

Then she put her glasses back on and reopened the book. Under different circumstances, I might have walked away. But she was young and pretty, and it wasn't hard to see how someone like her could work up a grudge against someone like Leon Ringold. I decided to give her one more try. I cleared my throat noisily and said, "Couldn't we start over again?"

"After all we've been through?" she said without looking up. "Let's stop kidding around. I know precisely why you're here. To spy for Ringold. And if you think I'm going to help you cut my own throat, you'd better think again. Anyway, I don't like your looks. We'd never get along."

"It's a good thing we didn't have kids, then, isn't it?"

She smiled into *The Women's Room*. Not a big grin, but a start.

I said, "Ringold aside, just what is it about me you don't like?"

"That's a bit like the joke about Mrs. Lincoln and the play, isn't it?" she said and closed the book. "Let's just say I don't trust Leon Ringold or anybody who works for him."

"What if I told you that I don't trust Ringold either?"

"You're taking his money, aren't you? You don't need to trust him."

She had a point. An insulting point, to be sure. But, then, she didn't know me; and men in my profession don't have reputations for virtue, if that's your idea of a reputation.

"I didn't ask for any help on this case," she said, eyeing me frostily. "And I don't need any macho cops coming around and queering it for me now."

I began to think she was right. We *wouldn't* ever get along. "Take another look, Ms. Davis," I said stiffly. "You'll notice that I'm not walking on my knuckles. And my brow may be a little craggy, but there's a decent brain behind it. You've got me all tagged and pigeon-holed before you've given me a chance to prove you're right. You call that fair?"

She glared at the floor for a second and thought it over. "All right, security consultant, what do you have to say?"

"Well, for starters, when I walked up here just now I wondered why you'd made yourself so visible. Sitting on a stool in front of the art shelf may scare this guy away for awhile, but the longer you stay here the more familiar you'll become. If the Hyde Park Ripper is a real psycho and he's still lurking around this place, he may start to make all kinds of unpleasant connections between you and the books you're guarding. He may even decide to follow you home one night with his trusty penknife."

"I'm counting on it," she said flatly.

That stopped me. Cold. I looked again at that pretty girl with the studious face and said, "You mean to say you're baiting him? You *want* him to come after you?"

She nodded. "I'm a third degree brown belt in karate, Mr. Stoner." She held up two pretty white hands. "In California, I'd have to register these as weapons."

I laughed. She sounded so damn silly I couldn't help it, although I could have bitten my tongue off afterward.

Kate Davis lowered her mitts and looked me squarely in the eyes. "You know there are all kinds of pigeon-holers and some of them ought to grow up and look around them. These are different times, Mr. Stoner. But, then, you wouldn't understand."

And with that she turned on her heels and walked away, down that dark aisle lined with oversized art books.

I'm not a particularly vain man, but I like to think I understand the etiquette of the eighties as well as the next he/she or "ter." If I err, it's usually on the side of caution; and I usually apologize for it when it's pointed out to me. But Ms. Davis was one of those arrogant young people who not only wants to point out your mistakes to you but to refuse all apologies. The kind who thinks that only she can see the rocks hidden in every snowball of a metaphor. With someone like that, male or female, etiquette goes out the window and I say, "Forget it."

All of which meant that she'd made me mad. Mad enough to act unprofessionally. Instead of asking her whether she'd checked out the list of names Ringold had given me or whether she'd consulted with the police, who keep tidy files on sex offenders, I stamped downstairs to the first floor reading room, plunked myself down in one of the nubby orange chairs they'd sunk beside the picture windows, and

11

stared at the cars nosing along Erie Avenue. Outside it was a beautiful fall day and, after a minute or two, I decided it was damn foolishness to waste it, brooding over Kate Davis. I'd do the job I was paid to do; and if the lady thought I was too much of an antique to deal with, that was too bad for the lady.

"Karate!" I said aloud.

And a sweet little voice replied: "It's not just a sport."

I looked up.

The owl-faced woman with the red cardigan sweater was standing in front of me.

I grinned at her. "What do you know about karate?"

"Oh," she said. "I know quite a number of odd facts. You can't work in a library for thirty years without picking up a great number of facts. One year I read all the way through 'R' in the *Encyclopaedia Brittanica*. I would say that I'm an expert on facts through 'R.'" She held out her hand and for a second I thought she expected me to kiss it. "I'm Jessie Moselle. Like the wine."

"Harry Stoner," I said.

"Oh, dear, that's an 'S,'" she said with alarm. "I don't know my 'S's.' It sounds like an English name, though. Randolph is an English name."

"Is it?" I said. "I believe I *am* part English. With a little Irish thrown in, too."

That pleased her. "Moselle is a German name. My parents were born in Lvov. That's in the Soviet Union, now. Of course, when they were born, it was part of Austria." She blinked once, very slowly, and said, "Davis is an English name."

"Indeed?"

"Oh, yes. Davis or Davies has quite a pedigree. Kate doesn't like me to mention it, but I once traced her family tree—that's a hobby of mine, tracing family trees—and she has a general in her past."

"Was he any good?"

"Yes, as a matter of fact, he was. He was rather impetuous, but he won many battles. He was a Leo. Kate is a Leo, too. Leo's are fiery, you know."

I liked Jessie Moselle. "And what sign are you?" I asked her.

"I'm a Sagittarius. Many philosophers were Sagittarians."

"I'm not surprised."

She smiled demurely. "I have to go, now. We're picking up reserves for visible shelving."

As she toddled off, I thought that the morning hadn't been a complete waste. I'd made one new friend. And now, I said to myself, as I got out of that surprisingly comfortable chair, it's time to look up an old one.

I drove west down Erie, that stately street full of red brick colonials and towering oaks, to Madison, where I turned south past the high-rises and the old yellow-brick apartments that are set above the boulevard on grassy slopes. Sun-burnt leaves were falling everywhere on the lawns and sidewalks. Red maples and orange oaks, shaped like hands, drifting down through the brisk October air, full of sunlight and the sound of the leaves in the wind. I felt like trailing a stick down those sidewalks and stirring the leaves into whirlwinds. Fall has that effect on a man not quite middle-aged. Or it has on this man. I guess I'm just not that far away from a kid with a stick. Especially on an October day with everything going to pieces of color, like a tinted mirror broken in the street.

But I didn't get out of the car and kick at the leaves. I did the manly thing, the adult thing, and went ahead with my business, although I did stay on Madison, taking the long way to town. Through the fringes of Hyde Park, where the beer barons had built their rococo mansions. Through East Walnut Hills, itself once a rich suburb and still populated on its fringes by white-collar types—the rebuilders, the FHA renovators who want to turn their little communities into walled islands with white sand beachheads. Drove back through successive layers of money and its subsidence, until I got to the part where the money just dried up and blew away. The place where it's burning summer all year round. McMillan Street. Peebles Corner. Looted during the '68 riots and never rebuilt. A little burnt-out spot about two miles square. One of several dozen in this city that no one will ever touch again. Not even with a stick on a crisp fall day. And from there, it was just a long roller-coaster ride down Gilbert Avenue to the city and to the fresh, highly visible cash that made the trip seem like coasting into a bank.

What they're doing to this city is a crime. The downtown money-men, I mean. With those magic wands that marbelize everything, turning good red brick into skyscrapers of polished stone and plate glass. Or maybe it isn't a crime. Maybe you're just getting old, I thought, and need something to feel bittersweet about on this fine fall day. Feeling nostalgic for demi-Gothic buildings and WPA frescoes didn't quite fit the bill. But, just the same, I was glad I was headed for the old Court House on the north side of town, well away from the part of the inner city that's been torn down and rebuilt.

Once I hit the east side, it only took me five minutes to work my way up Court Street to the square. I parked the Pinto on one of the visitor's stalls and walked up the steps to the Court House—a huge Greek-revival temple, decked with stirring mottoes and corinthian pilasters. Inside the lobby it was as cool and dark as a sick room. Well-fed lawyers passed mildly away, across Twelfth Street to the Traffic Court in the Alms & Doepke Building. I didn't see a familiar face until I got up to the fourth floor, and then it was all smiles and good cheer. I'd worked for the District Attorney's office for two years, right after I'd gotten out of the Army; and there were still enough old-timers around to make me feel at home. I slapped a few backs and pressed a few hands and kissed a secretary or two on the cheek and made a sweet, triumphant progress down the hallway to George DeVries's office.

You wouldn't have been able to tell it from his face—he looks like a carrot-topped Carl Sandburg—but George DeVries was and is a very brutal man. When he first came over to the D.A.'s office from Station X, it was rumored that he'd been shuffled backstairs to avoid a shooting board. At the time I didn't believe it. But that was more than a decade ago, and I was young and fresh out of the service and just not very smart about civilian police. It didn't seem possible to me, then, that a taciturn Southerner like George DeVries, with his weathered face and antebellum good manners, could have killed two black teenagers in an Avondale apartment house simply because one of the boys had refused to kick back some narcotics money. Twelve years have gone by and I've learned to suspend my disbelief about what other human beings are capable of doing in anger or in despair, although a part of me—the Cincinnati moralist side of Harry Stoner—can still get mightily outraged when appearances and realities drift too far apart. When they loose their moorings entirely, I become just as devoted to the cosmetics of the established order as the most pious burgher. Sometimes it's useful to pretend that the world ought to be a better place than it is, even if it is an imperative founded exclusively on schoolboy good wishes and the quirks of the subjunctive mood. Deep down, I didn't approve of George DeVries's brand of toughness. On the other hand, I knew that he was a smart, well-connected cop and that he still had friends on the vice squad. And you don't have to love a Chevrolet to catch a ride in one.

George was gazing out the window at the sunlit street when I came through the door.

"Beautiful day, huh?" I said to him.

He swiveled in his chair and looked up at me with surprise.

"Well, I'll be damned." He broke into a wrinkled grin. "Harry! How you been, boy? How's the world treating you?"

"Good, George. Real good."

"Take a seat," he said, sweeping his hand across the desk. "And tell me what's new."

I sat down and told him the news—about Ringold, the Hyde Park library, and the mutilated books. When I got to the books, he perked up.

"You know something I ought to hear, George?" I said to him.

He rubbed his chin savagely and said, "I'm not sure. Goddamn it, I must be getting old." He tapped his forehead as if he were trying to knock something inside back in place. "I may be wrong, but I think there's an open case of homicide from a couple of years back that could tie in with this business."

"A murder?"

"A real nasty murder, Harry. In Eden Park, I think."

Swell, I said to myself. "I guess you better find out for

16

sure, George. I didn't tell you this, but there's a crack girl detective on the case who thinks she can handle it all by herself."

"And just how the hell does she plan to do that?"

"With her hands, George," I said wearily. "With karate."

"Karate!" DeVries burst into laughter. "The guy we're talking about used a forty-ounce baseball bat and a barber's razor."

I reached into my sports coat and pulled out Ringold's list. "You'd better run makes on this crew, as well."

DeVries took the slip of paper and looked it over. "Nobody familiar here," he said.

"I didn't think there would be. But run them anyway. They're people who've taken out art books over the last couple of years. Maybe you'll get lucky and come up with a ringer."

"All right, Harry," he said. "I'll give you a call tonight or tomorrow about this. If you want the details of that homicide, you might go down to Central Station and talk with Al Foster."

"Thanks, George."

"Don't mention it," he said. "Things have been too damn slow around here to suit me."

I didn't share his enthusiasm.

3

THE CINCINNATI Police Building is located rather picturesquely on Ezzard Charles Drive, where it intersects Central Parkway on the northwest side of the city. Music Hall, red as a brick kiln and domed and gabled like a mosque, sits across the Parkway from it; and on its right, going south into town, is the sleek new building which houses the local public T.V. station. There is nothing sleek about the Police Building itself, which has the grim, foreshortened look of a fifties high school. But then the men who work there don't pay a hell of a lot of attention to the color of the walls. Which are yellow, by the way, the dull, penal yellow of glazed brick.

It took me about twenty minutes to drive over there, park, get cleared and tagged by one of the desk sergeants, and locate Lieutenant Alvin Foster, who was manning a desk in a spare dry-walled office on the second floor and not looking terribly happy about it. Al Foster seldom looks happy about anything. He is one of the least congenial men I've ever known. Between the cigarettes that dangle from his lips like a second tongue, his long dour Buster Keaton-like face, and the thatch of greasy black hair on the top of his head, he does not make a good first impression. But he's not interested in good; he's interested in lasting. And in that respect he always succeeds. I'd known him for better than a year, ever since the Hugo Cratz case. And while we were hardly close friends, we did do some friendly drinking together.

He had a cigarette in his mouth, as usual. When he spotted me coming through the door, he made a stab at a smile, landing somewhere on my side of bare tolerance.

"Harry," he said in his high-pitched, achy voice.

And I said, "Al. How you been?"

"Oh, you know."

And that was it.

I sat down on a padded metal chair across from his desk, and for a minute or two we didn't say anything. He just sat there with blue smoke crawling up his face, brooding over his desk as if he'd lost the key to the top drawer. And I examined a discolored spot on my thumbnail and stared out the window at the autumn sky.

"You need some help, Harry?" he said after a time.

I gave it a beat or two and said, "Yeah, Al. I could use some help."

He snapped the cigarette he'd been smoking into a tin ashtray, where it continued to burn, dug into his rumpled black coat, and pulled another Tareyton from his pocket like a magician plucking a dove from his sleeve.

"Got a light?"

I gave him a light.

"Yeah," he said and picked at a loose strand of tobacco on his lip. "You were saying?"

"You know, Al," I said to him. "You're a fun guy."

"Thanks, Harry. That means a lot to me, your saying that."

I laughed. "I need some information. George DeVries over at the D.A.'s office seems to remember an open case of homicide from about two years ago. Up in Eden Park. A real messy killing with a razor."

"Belton," he said and looked at the cigarette. "Twyla Belton."

We sat in silence for another minute and I finally said, "All right, Al. I'll bite. Twyla Belton who?"

"Why do you ask, Harry?"

I told him. Why not? There was nothing confidential about what I'd been hired to do. And even if there had been, I would have spilled most of it eagerly.

Foster listened to me without looking up, stubbed out his cigarette, pulled out another and said, "So what? So somebody's tearing up a few books."

"The Belton thing wasn't my idea, Al. It was DeVries who saw a connection. I told you my story, now you tell me about Twyla."

"Not much to tell," he said. "Female. Cauc. About twenty-three. Was a student at Lon Aamons' commercial art school in Walnut Hills. No known enemies. You know —just your standard single girl. We found her body on the Overlook about two years ago." He flicked the ash off his cigarette. "She'd been worked over bad."

"How bad?"

"Let me put it this way, Harry. Don't ask where we found the bat."

"Good Lord," I said softly and shuddered up and down my spine. "Did you have any leads?"

"Not a one. She just wasn't a real likely target for that kind of thing. No boyfriends. Shy. Just a girl who went up to the park on the wrong day. The guy she ran into . . ." Foster shifted in his chair and looked up at me for the first time since I'd sat down. "I'd like to meet him sometime."

And I'd bet he would, too. "I don't remember anything about this in the papers. Why'd you put a lid on it?"

"Figure it out for yourself," he said daintily. "Dead girl. Sexually molested and then cut to ribbons. No motive. No suspects."

I saw what he meant. "So you thought you were up against a real psycho."

He nodded. "Those guys love publicity. And you know the kind of panic a newspaper story can start. What we did was dress up some of our policewomen as marks and quadruple the patrols at municipal parks. But the son-of-a-bitch never showed up again. He just vanished."

"That's strange," I said. "You'd have thought he'd keep at it until he got caught."

Foster grunted.

"Where'd the girl live?" I asked him.

"On Paxton."

"That's in Hyde Park."

"So?"

He was right. It wasn't very much.

"She have a family?"

"Father and mother."

We sat for a few moments more in silence.

21

"You might let me know if you find anything interesting," he said laconically.

"You figure I'm going to follow up on this, huh?"

"You're the type," Al said.

An awful lot of people know your type, Harry, I said to myself, as I walked back to the car. Which is what? Out of touch? Hopelessly old-fashioned? Naively sentimental? All of the above?

Chances were that there was nothing to the Belton connection. Crazies generally don't turn to books *after* they've torn up real people. But there was a correlation—a similarity. And the girl had lived in Hyde Park. And, anyway, I'm the suspicious type. On the way down to the Riorley Building I decided to check with Ringold to find out whether Twyla Belton had belonged to the Hyde Park Library. And if so, just what kind of books she'd liked to read.

There weren't any messages for me on the answerphone in my office. So I went down to the lobby coffee shop and had a sandwich with Jim Dugan, a lawyer with offices on the sixth floor of the Riorley. He was still upset about Pete Rose and Dick Wagner. Before he signed with the Phillies, two years ago, a motion was made in city council to have Pete named a municipal monument. That way, it was argued, the Reds would have had to sign him, since the citizens of Cincinnati would have been picking up the tab for maintenance of city property. I suppose you've got to like Cincinnatians just for that. They're small-minded and drab and about as hopelessly parochial as any large group of people can be, but they elected Carl Klinger mayor after he was caught in a Newport brothel and they tried to make Pete Rose into a city park. You explain it.

22

About five o'clock I left Jim to his dark mood and took mine home with me to Clifton and the Delores—the four-story, U-shaped brownstone apartment house I've lived in for the past ten years. I drove out Reading Road because I didn't want to see what was left of that Monday afternoon through the smog that hangs over the expressway. But smog or no smog, the day had lost some of its luster—its freshness all mixed up with torn pages and a murdered girl and a smart-ass lady detective who'd gotten my dander up. And all of a sudden I realized that I'd found that something to mourn over I'd been looking for since the start of the day. It wasn't anything new. Just one almost-middle-aged and generally-well-meaning man, who'd discovered for the umpteenth time that he couldn't even make it through a beautiful fall afternoon without stepping in it. *It.* The stuff that most people's bad dreams are made of, which he tracked around like fresh mud on his shoes. It's enough to drive that man to drink, I thought. So I turned west on Taft and drove myself to the Busy Bee and drank.

The Scotch which I'd drunk neat at the dark, horseshoe-shaped bar left me feeling warm and lucid and just a bit out of kilter, as if my joints weren't quite tight enough or my skin too loose. Anyway, I was feeling fine and silly when I stepped into my two-and-a-half room apartment at about nine-thirty that night. I kicked at a Gold Toe sock that had found its way into the living room, switched the Zenith Globemaster to WGN in Chicago, made myself comfortable on my green plaid couch, and thought about Pete Rose and Dick Wagner and Three Mile Island and the Arab shiekdoms and the cost of gas and a very nice-looking blonde girl I'd seen at the Bee.

I was just drifting off into a fat, alcoholic sleep when the phone rang. It got me up too quickly, and I sat back down hard. All that sweet, musical liquor was starting to boil, and suddenly I didn't feel so dreamy and good-tempered. I worked my way like a blind man to the roll-top desk beneath the front window and picked up the receiver.

"Mr. Stoner?" a husky, familiar voice said.

"A piece of him."

"Kate Davis, here. I hope I didn't wake you up."

I glanced at my watch, which was showing a little past ten, and did a slow burn. "You figure a man of my years needs his sleep, is that right, Ms. Davis?"

She laughed prettily. "Not exactly. I just thought you might turn in early like I usually do. After a day's work, I'm bushed. And I owe it to myself and the job to be as fresh as possible in the morning."

My right hand began to tremble and I eyed it with horror. I couldn't tell if it was the liquor or Kate Davis, who had a very nice talent for saying the wrong things. "I'll bet you're a vegetarian, too," I said with spite.

"As a matter of fact," she said equably, "I eat just about anything. Within reason. The only vanity I deny myself is liquor."

"It figures."

"Oh, it's not as though I'm morally opposed to it. Hell, I'd go out every night and get as stewed as a Detroit assembly-line worker, if it weren't for the job."

"Well, it's nice to have ideals," I said, suddenly feeling very drunk and very old.

"I have to have them," she said. "Especially on a job like this one. You see, most people feel as you do—that the security business is not 'woman's work.'"

"It was swell of you to call like this," I said. "I mean I don't get to talk to a lot of young people. But it's getting way past my bedtime, so if you wouldn't mind getting to the point . . .?"

"Listen," she said. "What I wanted to say can wait till tomorrow."

"Noooo. Let's not wait until tomorrow. I may not be alive tomorrow."

"Are you O.K.?" she said with concern. "You're not sick, are you?"

"Just what do you want!" I almost shouted.

There was a pause, then she said, "To work together?" in a very small voice.

I didn't say anything.

"Jessie told me about the meeting you had with Ringold," she said sheepishly. "And some friends of mine told me that . . . well, that you know what you're doing."

I started to ask her how Jessie Moselle had known about that conversation, but let it slide.

She took a deep breath and said, "Could be I was wrong about you."

"You mean I'm not as venal and sexist as you thought?"

"Could be," she said.

"And how would our little partnership work?" I said with morbid fascination. "What would we do—split shifts on that stool of yours?"

"It doesn't have to be that way," she said defensively. "I'm open to suggestions. We could pool our information."

"All right," I said. "Then let me do some pooling right now. About two years ago a twenty-four-year-old girl named Twyla Belton was brutally murdered in Eden Park.

25

She was cut up like one of those art books of yours. And the guy who did it was never found."

"What makes you think her death has anything to do with the library?"

"It doesn't have to have anything to do with the library. She was from Hyde Park, but that doesn't necessarily mean a thing. The point I'm trying to make is that, whether or not our Ripper killed Twyla Belton, he could be capable of killing. And sitting on that chair of yours and practically inviting him home, just doesn't make good sense."

"You think I should be scared," she said stiffly.

And I realized that I *had* scared her and that I'd wanted to scare her. It made me feel like a bully playing a cruel game, but it was somehow comforting to know that behind that sexual armor she was capable of a healthy fright. Most people with a point to prove give up their feelings because they think that having feelings makes them weak. Some of them give up feeling for the rest of their lives. It was nice to know that Kate Davis wasn't one of that clan.

"Not scared," I said. "But wary."

I tried to sound conciliatory, but I'd knicked her pride the way she'd knicked mine earlier in the day. And she didn't want me to know it.

"This girl, Twyla Belton," she said in a businesslike voice. "Did she belong to the library?"

It was a smart question, one I'd wondered about myself. "We'll check it out," I said.

"It would be interesting," she said. "If she were on Ringold's list."

"She probably won't be on the list. The Belton girl was killed over two years ago and I don't think Ringold went back that far. We'll just have to do some digging."

"All right," she said. "Then I'll see you tomorrow."

26

"Yes. See you tomorrow."

"Bright and early?"

"Jesus," I said.

She laughed. "Try a raw egg in a glass of tomato juice with a dash of Tabasco." And she hung up, leaving me wondering vaguely just who had been playing games with whom.

4

I woke up feeling as if someone had tied sandbags to my hair.

Just lie still, I told myself. Lie still and it will all go away. The Globemaster was playing a raucous Von Suppé overture, and one little ray of sunlight had found its way through the thick folds of the bedroom curtains and was creeping slowly up the blanket toward my face. I couldn't have been more delighted if it were a tarantula, moving on eight woolly legs.

I threw off the covers and sat up. Very quickly. Something inside my head shifted like water in a fifty-gallon cooler and kept lapping against my skull—back and forth, back and forth—until I made myself stand up and it turned into a lump of red-hot stone.

I managed to shower. Water is soft. But I didn't trust myself around fire or earth until I'd towelled dry and started to dress. It was exactly nine o'clock when I put the coffee on the stove and nine-ten when I found the nerve to shave. It was almost nine-thirty when I found that other Gold Toe sock, nestling like a kitten under the couch. I slipped it on my foot, stepped into my shoes, pulled a gray wool sports coat from the hall rack, and hobbled out the door.

It was four flights to the lobby—some sixty steps—where the glass door was lit up like a motion picture screen before the projector is loaded with film. Just one white-hot square of light. The fourth element and the cruelest. Out I went, into what was possibly a beautiful Tuesday morning, as clean as new shoes. Sneaked quickly past the dogwoods in the front yard but still caught their scent, like smelling toothpaste on somebody's breath. Walked around the south side of the building to the lot. Went down four concrete steps, got into the Pinto, flipped on the ignition— said, "Good, Harry. Good."—and pulled out.

My head and stomach felt a little better by the time I got to Hyde Park, where the towering oaks hid the sun and Erie Avenue was as cool, green, and peaceful as the bed of a forest. I would have felt better still if I hadn't known exactly what was waiting for me at the library. And I wasn't thinking of Ringold, either. It was the girl. Oh, God, I thought miserably, I know how it's going to be. After all, I was young once—for a few hours the day before I'd been no more than eight—and full of enthusiasms, eager to test

29

myself against the old hands, to prove my mettle, to earn my wings. Red badge of courage. *Croix de guerre.* Oh, God, I thought.

And, of course, I was right.

She greeted me at the door like a bellhop—"Bag, mister?" All blonde and pink and tipped with carmine red. She smelled of toothpaste. And talc. And something sweeter than lilacs. And she looked healthier than a Vic Tanney bathing beauty and just as pretty as the fall day in her burnt-orange suit. When she started waving a sheaf of papers at me, I said, "No! Enough!"

Her face fell. "I thought we had an agreement," she said.

And I said, "We do. Only not now."

She smiled. "You want some aspirin?"

"Please."

She started off for the front desk, turned back and said, "Ringold's looking for you."

"He can reach me at that chair," I said, pointing to a spot beneath one of the picture windows.

I walked over to the chair and sat down. Kate Davis brought me an aspirin. Miss Moselle brought me some water in a dixie cup. And they both stood over me while I took my medicine.

"It's not the alcohol alone," Miss Moselle said judiciously, "that causes a hangover. No, indeed. It is impurities in the grain that produce many of the symptoms. Of course, alcohol does dehydrate the system, disturbing the electrolyte balance. And it is, as well, a mild toxin. Thus the feverish feeling. The body aches. Sweating. And chills."

"Wonderful," I said.

"I myself," said Miss Moselle, "prefer Bushnell's Irish whiskey, because of its peaty flavor."

Kate Davis said, "Better not mention whiskey again, Jess."

Miss Moselle put a hand to her mouth and said, "Oh." She had a lace handkerchief tucked in the sleeve of her sweater, which made me think of my own grandmother and her handkerchiefs and sachets. "I have a small bottle of spirits of ammonia in my purse," she said thoughtfully. "If you would care for a mild stimulant?"

"No, I'm fine," I said, smiling at both of them. "I'm feeling much better."

Miss Moselle gave me a tender look and glanced at the girl. "I have work to do," she said and walked away.

"I think she's leaving us to ourselves," Kate Davis said with high seriousness.

"Very courteous."

"More than that. She expects us to fall in love."

"You're kidding?" I said.

"Nope," she said. "She's got her heart set on it."

"Why?"

Kate looked up at the ceiling. "The stars," she said mysteriously. "Jess does my horoscope daily. It's another one of her hobbies. And she assures me that Venus is in the ascendant. Forgive me for asking you this, but I promised Jess." She screwed her face up daffily and said, "What sign are you?"

"Scorpio. But I'm on the cusp."

"I'll relay the news. Meanwhile . . ." She pulled that sheaf of papers out again. "I have some news for you. I have been very busy this morning."

"I figured."

"Why do you say that so balefully?" she said. "Youth must have its day."

31

The June and December thing was beginning to rankle me. And I think she knew it. "Just how the hell old are you anyway?" I asked her.

"Twenty-five. And you?"

"Old," I said.

"You're thirty-seven," Kate Davis said triumphantly. "Jess looked at your green card."

"My green card?"

"It's Ringold's system. Green is for part-time employees. I'm a blue card. That is, until Ringold can figure out a way to get rid of me."

"So what is that stack of papers?" I said.

"Research. You'll be pleased to learn that Twyla Belton was, indeed, a customer here. And her specialty was history books."

"How did you find that out?"

"By digging," she said. "They reshelved most of the history books two years ago and a lot of the older ones are downstairs in storage. I just went through the withdrawal cards in the back of a few of the stored books and found her name."

"That's damn good," I said. "I don't know what it proves. But it's damn good."

"It proves our friend the Ripper could have seen Twyla here," she said a bit defensively. "Two years ago, the history books were shelved near the art section. He could have seen her here as he worked."

"It's a possibility."

Someone called my name from the front desk.

I looked up. Ringold was gesturing impatiently from the door of his office.

"Duty calls," I said to Kate.

32

She looked me over carefully. "I hope I'm not making a mistake with you."

"Youth must be taught," I said and walked up to the desk.

Ringold was on the phone when I entered his office. He was holding the receiver to his nose and talking into it with a brisk, affected good humor. He waved to me and I sat down. Leon Ringold was one of those people who make the same gestures over the phone that they make in face-to-face conversation. He rolled his eyes, pleaded with his hands, and puckered his lips as if he were reciting the French vowels. When he caught me staring at him, he turned in his chair. By the end of the call, he'd covered his face with one hand at the brow.

He put the phone in the cradle and continued to cover his face, as if it were the most natural thing in the world to look like you had a splitting headache.

"You know, Stoner," he said in a peevish voice, "when I said you should talk with Ms. Davis, I had not intended that you make a habit of it."

"I'll keep it in mind," I said.

"Well, have you anything to report?" he said and began to lower his hand. The whole routine was beginning to remind me of the contortions people go through when they don't want to look foolish after tripping.

"Not yet. I gave your list of names to a friend at the D.A.'s office. He's going to see if any of them are known sexual offenders. There is also a very remote possibility that your vandal may have been involved in a more violent crime."

"Good heavens!" he said and dropped his hand to the desk. "What kind of crime?"

"I'd rather tell you when I'm sure he's the same man. Right now I'd just be making a wild guess."

"Look here," he said. "I'm paying you. I have the right to know these things."

I guessed he thought that Kate Davis was piping all her secrets to his rival, Joffrey, and he didn't want to be left behind in the race. So I told him about Twyla Belton, and his face turned white.

"That's disgusting," Ringold said. "I don't want to hear any more of that sort of speculation."

"You asked," I reminded him.

He stared at me coldly and raised his voice a notch. "You are working for me, Stoner. Don't forget it. And as far as I'm concerned, we're hunting for a vandal. If you want to go searching for sex murderers—if that tickles your detective's ego—well, you just do it on your own time."

"Is that it?" I said, getting up from the chair.

"Not quite." He picked up a piece of notepaper and handed it to me. "This man called earlier this morning. When you were . . . indisposed."

I glanced at the note. George DeVries had called at ten-thirty. He'd left his extension and asked me to return the call.

"All right." I folded up the note. "Can I use the phone?"

"I suppose." Ringold got up from his desk.

"Remember what I told you about Ms. Davis," he said as he walked from the room.

5

I DIALED the number written on the note paper and got transferred to a second extension—some inner, inner sanctum of the old Court House—and after holding for a minute or so, finally got through to George DeVries.

"What's up?" I asked him.

"I think I have a hot one for you, Harry boy," he said cheerfully. "Right off the top of that list of yours. A guy named Leo Sachs. Turns out he was hauled into Station Six about three years ago for indecent exposure."

"Was he charged?" I said.

"Uh-uh," DeVries said. "His neighbor got cold feet and refused to prosecute."

"You have any details?"

"Just the arresting officer's report."

I picked up a pencil from a cannister on Ringold's desk and said, "Give."

"A patrol car was summoned to the neighbor's residence at 11:30 P.M., May 17, 1978. The neighbor, a guy named Segal, claimed that Sachs had exposed himself earlier that evening. A friend of Segal's, a woman named Nellie Silas, corroborated his testimony. Sachs was pinched and taken to the Hyde Park station, booked, and released when Segal refused to press charges."

"You got an address on Sachs?"

"2603 Delta Avenue. But I don't know if that's current."

"O.K. What about a description?"

DeVries made an apologetic noise, like a cough at a concert. "That's the bad news. This guy Sachs is in his early seventies."

"For chrissake!" I said.

"All right," DeVries said. "So he's not a bat-wielder. But he sure as hell could be the guy *you're* looking for."

Of course, he was right. And I was a little ashamed of myself for having felt disappointed. Ringold may not be far wrong about you, I thought. That ego of yours may *not* be satisfied with a simple vandal. Which was a moderately chilling discovery.

I thanked DeVries for the help and told him I'd check Sachs out.

"Glad to lend a hand," he said. "I sure hope he's the one you want, because the other folks on that list are as normal as white bread."

I hung up the phone and walked out to the service area behind the check-out desk, where Miss Moselle was standing in front of a wooden file, sorting through catalogue cards. I didn't see Kate Davis around.

36

"Miss Moselle?" I said. "Do you know a man named Leo Sachs?"

She stopped sorting the cards and said, "Oh my, yes. He's that big, ruddy gentleman with gray hair and a very loud voice. Is he a suspect?"

"What do you think?"

She deliberated for a second. "Well, we did have some trouble with him two summers ago. He'd come into our periodical room and read *Die Freiheit* out loud. It was most disconcerting to the other patrons. Eventually, Mr. Ringold had to ask him to leave. Yes, I suppose he could be a suspect," she admitted.

"But you wouldn't put him at the top of your list?"

She bit her lip and blinked solemnly. "I rather think not. He's really a sweet man, despite his bluster. Or so he appears to me. But then I'm far from an expert on sexual deviants. The 'S's', you know."

"Maybe we could use an expert," I said. "A clinical psychologist, perhaps."

She shrugged. "I have no faith in modern psychology. I believe in the theory of the four humors. And, of course, in the stars."

"So you'd recommend an astrologer?"

"I know several very good ones," she said earnestly. "In fact, if I were you, I'd keep my eye peeled for a choleric fellow with a saturnine disposition."

It sounded like me.

"Maybe I'd better pay Sachs a visit, just in case."

"I'll tell Kate where you're going, then," she said pleasantly.

Leo Sachs lived in an apartment complex on Delta Avenue about two blocks north of Mt. Lookout square. It was one of those new developments that look something like piles of derailed boxcars—squat brown buildings angled about a central court and the whole shebang stuck on a grassy slope and called "The Nest" or "The Chalet" or whatever fashionable name the developer decides to slap on its back. This one was known as "Le Village," and it looked expensive.

I parked on Delta beneath a blood-red maple and walked up a long concrete stairway to the apartment complex. A kid with stringy brown hair, wire rims, and a wispy moustache—like those moustaches you see in Chinese miniatures, the ones where you can count every hair on two hands—was raking leaves beneath a redbud. He seemed to be more interested in making designs than in getting the job done, which made me think that he might belong to the place or to one of the families in it. He was wearing a red-plaid lumberjack shirt and faded denim jeans and looked like a gypsy who had been kidnapped by merchants when he was a baby.

I walked up to him and said, "Hi."

He said "Hi" back and continued to make lazy S's in the leaves.

"You live here?"

He nodded gravely and stirred the leaves with his spoon. He wasn't a talker, this kid. But then I guess I didn't look as if I had much to say that would interest him. I asked him if he knew a Mr. Sachs and, for some reason, *that* got his attention.

He planted the rake at his side, leaned on the handle and eyed me suspiciously. "Are you here to make trouble, mister?" he said in a snippety little boy's voice. He looked me over a second time and said, "You're with the I.R.S., aren't you? You're going to try to cheat that old man out of a few more dollars."

It sounded like something he'd overheard at the dinner table. Which meant that Leo Sachs was one of those amiable old men who've become community property, like scruffy dogs. Everybody's meat.

"Just tell me where he lives, O.K.?"

"Find it yourself," the kid said and went back to work with a vengeance.

I looked at him a minute and said, "What the hell." And off I went to find Leo Sachs.

His name wasn't listed on the shiny brass mailboxes of the first apartment house in "Le Village" complex. Or on the second. But the third was the charm. Leo Sachs. Number Seven.

I walked through the glass entry door and down a narrow hall that smelled vaguely like a hospital corridor of disinfectant and overheated air. There was a brass buzzer on the door of Number Seven. I pressed it and waited—a long time—until I heard somebody fiddling with the chain. The door opened a crack and a hearty, thickly accented male voice said, "What is it you want?"

"Mr. Sachs?" I said.

"Yeah. I am Sachs."

"My name's Stoner. Could I talk to you?"

"No," he said with great finality and slammed the door shut.

I pressed the buzzer again.

"You go away," Leo Sachs said from behind the door. "You go away or I'll phone the police."

I hated to do it, but I had the feeling it was the only way, short of a subpoena, that I was going to get in. So I cleared my throat and said, "I *am* the police," in my deepest, most authoritative voice.

It worked.

He said, "You are the police?" And I heard the chain sliding out of the catch. The door opened wide. "Why don't you say you are the police in the first place?" Leo Sachs said with offended dignity. "You should say this when you ring. Then I would open the door."

He was a huge, robust man. About as big as I am. With a square, ruddy face and short-cropped gray hair and the kind of bull neck that terminates in rolls of flesh at the nape. He looked, for all the world, like an Ashkenazic Victor McLaughlin. A big, ham-fisted old man in a white dress shirt and black suspenders, with round, frameless spectacles on his nose.

"So come in," he said and showed me through the door into a living room that was all polished mahogany and pile rugs. Sideboards, secretaries, cabinets that had the gloss of patent leather and smelled of lemon oil.

Sachs lowered himself into a wing-back chair with a crotcheted cushion and pointed to a small armchair beside him.

"Sit," he said.

I sat.

There was an octagonal table between us with a crusty pipe rack on its top. Sachs pulled a meerschaum from the rack and scoured the bowl with his thumb.

"So?" he said. "What can I do for you?"

I'd already lied about being a cop, so there was no sense in playing it any other way. I flashed my detective's license at him took a notepad from my coat pocket, flipped it open, and pretended to read nonchalantly from a blank page.

"You belong to the Hyde Park library, Mr. Sachs?"

"Sure. Yes."

He'd gotten that pipe going and his words came out in

puffs of cherry-flavored smoke. Between the lemon wax and the pipe tobacco, it was beginning to smell like a burning orchard in his room, which was heavily draped and carpeted and very hot. I explained the situation to him, trying to make it appear as if the interview were part of a larger investigation. When I mentioned the damaged books and the fact that he had taken some of those books out, he began to puff out smoke like a smudge pot. And when I got to the part about his police record, he exploded. Literally. Spewing sparks and ashes over his clothes and over the chair.

"When will you people stop tormenting me about this!" he said in an agonized voice. "How many times must I explain? That *shtarker* Segal is going to kill me with his lies."

His face was livid. The wattles of flesh about his neck had actually expanded, like a cobra's hood, and one of his cloudy blue eyes had become slightly unmoored. For a brief second, I thought he was about to have a stroke. Since all I was really interested in was clearing up the indecent exposure business, I made soothing noises and asked him gently if he wouldn't like to explain what had really happened. He nodded violently.

"I have a car," he said angrily. "This car—for thirty-four years I have driven this car. Not one accident. Not one!"

I told him that was commendable and he snorted with disgust.

"Wait!" he said. "Wait 'til you hear! Two years ago I moved to this building. It's a little more money, but what the hell, I deserved it. I worked hard. Thirty years I was a butcher. My own meat market in Avondale. I figured I deserved it. The pool. The sauna. Nice location, too. Right?"

41

"Right," I said.

"Wrong!" he exploded. "One afternoon, three years ago, I'm coming home from downtown. Every Saturday I go downtown. I shop Shillito's. I eat at the Cricket. Like clockwork. So I'm coming home and I see this *shtarker* Segal, who can't hardly walk, standing by the driveway. Sixty-two and he can't walk! Like a baby. He's standing on the sidewalk by the driveway. I honk at him and he waves like 'Go ahead.' So I pull in. Only as I pull in, he falls across the hood. I didn't hit him. How could I hit him? I'm only going maybe two miles an hour. I'm telling you, he *falls* across the hood! I stopped. Sure, I stopped. Got out. I say, 'Segal, what's the matter with you? Are you sick?' 'You hit me,' he says. 'I'll sue.' 'So, sue,' I tell him. What the hell do I care if he sues? The man's crazy. From generations back. Who'll believe him? A man never has an accident in his life is suddenly going to go crashing into people who can't even walk!

"Only your friends—the policemen—don't see it that way. Segal makes a complaint. They come out. I tell them exactly what happened. And before I can park the car, they say I'm to blame. That it's my fault Segal can't stay on his feet! A man who can't even stand up has got the right of way before a man never even got a parking ticket. Do I complain? No. I got insurance. I got coverage. Fifty-dollar deductible. So I got cheated. Listen, *boy-chik*, you can't live seventy-four years and not get cheated. I go inside. Drink some wine. Call my agent. And I figure that's the end of it. Only that's not the end."

"No?" I said.

Sachs snorted again. "This *shtarker* Segal gets a lawyer named Kraus. Belonged to the Bund, this Kraus. A Nazi. He gets Segal a doctor. The doctor says Segal has a slipped disk from where he fell on my hood. I'm going one-and-a-

42

half miles an hour and he's got a slipped disk! Segal comes to my apartment and says, 'I been to the doctor. He says I got to go to French Lick for the waters.' I say, 'French Lick is in Indiana. Why not some place close?' He says, 'It's got to be French Lick. For the waters.' I say, 'My insurance won't pay for that.' And he says, 'The waters or I sue.' So I call up my agent and he says, 'They got you over a barrel. It'll cost you more in court than to send the *shtarker* to Indiana.' I say, 'That's not fair.' He says, 'Fair ain't in the law books. Pay up.' What am I going to do?"

"Did you pay him?" I asked him.

"Sure, I paid. But that night . . ." Sachs held up one finger and smiled. "That night I went down the hall to Segal's apartment and I knocked on the door. At first he won't open it because he's afraid I'm going to punch him. 'What do you want?' he says. He says, 'Talk to my lawyer.' I say, 'Who needs lawyers? You win. I'll give you the waters.' So he opens the door and I unbutton my fly and—"

I started to laugh. "You didn't?"

"Sure I did," Leo Sachs said triumphantly. "I gave him the waters. I pissed all over his goddamn rug."

I laughed so hard that Sachs started to laugh too. "And *that's* why you were arrested?"

He nodded. "Segal said I exposed myself. Some woman in his apartment—his cousin, I think—she says she seen me do it."

"For chrissake!"

We kept laughing for another minute. And between the smoke and the laughter, my eyes started to tear. "Mr. Sachs," I said to him, "I'm sorry. I wouldn't have bothered you if I'd known the details."

"Oh, it's all right," he said, tamping his pipe. "Only next time, tell your friends, O.K.?"

"I promise."

I got up from the chair and wiped my eyes.

"About those books," he said. "They're ruined?"

"I'm afraid so."

"That's terrible!" Sachs said. He looked at me sympathetically. "Listen. If I tell you something else you won't say I said it?"

"Tell me what?" I said.

"Because I don't want no more cops coming to my door."

"All right," I said. "I give you my word. No more cops."

He tapped his pipe on a glass ash tray. "Two, three years ago," he said, lowering his voice, "I seen some kid cutting up a book."

I stopped wiping my eyes and looked at Sachs as if I were seeing him for the first time. "What kid?" I said.

"Some kid. It was in the john. On the second floor. I walk into a stall and there's a kid with a book on his lap and a razor blade. I say to him, 'What are you doing?' And he slams the door. What am I going to do? Push the toilet door open?"

"What did he look like?" I said. "How old was he?"

"A kid," Sachs said. "Maybe twenty, twenty-five. Just a kid."

"Would you recognize him again if you saw him?"

Sachs shook his head. "Three seconds—that's how long I saw him. And he had his head bent down."

"Did you report him to the librarian?" I asked.

Sachs flushed slightly and said, "I didn't want to get him in trouble."

"Look, Mr. Sachs," I said. "This could be very important. If I was to bring you some photographs or drawings, do you think you might be able to identify this boy's face?"

"I only saw him for two seconds," he said helplessly. "And this is years ago."

44

"Would you look anyway?"

"Sure, I'd look," he said. "But don't expect nothing."

I wanted to tell him that he'd already given me a lot more than I'd expected. But he'd had enough of private detectives for one afternoon. I thanked him for his help, apologized again for bothering him, and walked back out into the brisk fall air.

6

One summer, not too long ago, I was invited to join in a symposium at Oberlin University on "Investigative Techniques in Police Work." Of course I was flattered by the invitation, but eventually I turned it down. Partly because I don't enjoy lectures and lecturers and partly because I had the feeling that nobody at this conference would be particularly pleased with what I had to say. The symposium was designed for the high-powered techno-freaks, the gadget gang who are into computer-assisted analysis and voice-printing and galvanic skin measurement, as if criminal investigation were just another way of dissecting a frog.

Now I have very few illusions left about my work or about my life and, on most days, am willing to acknowledge that being happy in your work or happy about anything is mostly a matter of self-deception. Nevertheless, I get on with the job, which is rarely pleasant and sometimes more unpleasant than you can imagine. I do it because it's what I do best, what I have a talent for. And by God, I'm not willing to bend that talent to any computer analyst's prejudices.

I started to write it down—what I would say to that symposium crowd. Of course, I ended up writing an apology for my life, full of arrows and dots that all pointed shamelessly back to me. And I realized that what I was trying to get at was the nature of jobs themselves—how we appropriate and become them, the way a bird or an insect becomes a part of his surroundings. It seemed to me, then, that vocations were a kind of camouflage that most people evolved throughout a lifetime of little hurts and little triumphs, spun out of themselves the way a spider spins its web. And that for me, with my ingrown passion for finding things out, the job was no more or less than my way of tackling the mystery of knowing anyone at all. That, in spite of the cynical cracks, mine was essentially a lively business and, deep down, a moral art.

Now, who in that crowd would have listened to that kind of thing with a straight face? For that matter, who can listen to it now? And, yet, it's true, shameless, and very possibly absurd. But it helps to explain why I left Sachs feeling elated and to point up how much of that elation was a self-congratulatory pleasure in my work. Realistically I knew that it was pure chance that Leo Sachs happened to be in the second-floor john when my Ripper was at work.

And it was most certainly an accident, and a piece of outright cheek, that I'd come to Sachs in the first place. And yet I wasn't denying the accidental quality, just adding to it a kind of serendipitous contentment—the way you feel when you go back over a letter or a report you've written and discover that it's phrased more clearly than you thought at the time you wrote it.

What the hell, I said to myself, as I walked down the concrete stairs to Delta Avenue. Why not just admit it? After thirty-seven years, it's still all a mystery to you. Accidental or intentional, unexpected or predictable, it still comes as a surprise. But that's the advantage of not growing too far up, of not looking too critically into your own mechanisms. Like the monkey who presses the button and gets his banana—it was that kind of circuitous satisfaction I was feeling. And, of course, I knew immediately where to go next.

Back to the Hyde Park library, which was gleaming like a chrome fender in the afternoon sun. I parked the Pinto in the little asphalt lot beside the rear door, got out, still feeling lucky, and walked up to the glass entryway.

Inside it was already beginning to look like night. The fluorescent lights were taking hold, drying out the color of the carpeting and of clothes and the woody sheen of the big card catalogues next to the door. I waved to Miss Moselle, who was perched like a night owl on a stool behind the circulation desk, and walked up the staircase to the second floor. I'd started back to the art section on the east wall when someone called my name.

"Mr. Stoner?"

I turned around and saw that the gray-haired woman behind the Juvenile Desk was smiling at me. She had lipstick on her teeth and just about everywhere else beneath her nose; but she was jolly-looking in her loose print dress cinched at the waist with one of those perforated plastic belts that are made to fit any size. I smiled back at her and she said, "Were you looking for Kate?"

"As a matter of fact, yes."

"I thought so."

She held out a chubby pink hand. There was a slip of paper in it. "She told me to give this to you, if you came in."

I plucked the paper out of her hand as if I were plucking it out of a piece of risen dough, smiled at her again because she was so obviously expecting a reward, and walked over to one of the window chairs looking out on Erie Avenue. It was beginning to irritate me that so many people seemed to be in on my case. I mean Kate Davis was one thing. In a sense, I figured I was in on her case. But Miss Moselle and her coterie of old ladies was something else. And it wasn't simply a question of my professional pride being hurt, although if I'd been being very frank with myself I suppose that would have been a good deal of it. It was a question of safety, too. In spite of the cockamamie way the library was run, the Ripper thing wasn't just another piece of gossip. He was a proven vandal and potential dynamite. And the old ladies should have known that. Ringold should have known it. And so should Kate Davis. Who, the note informed me, had walked the three blocks to Paxton Avenue to talk with Twyla Belton's parents.

I had the feeling that Kate Davis liked the Belton connection a little too well, that, like a cub reporter or a rookie cop, she wasn't going to be satisfied with the slightly crazy kid Leo Sachs had helped me come up with. Now that I knew his approximate age, he could be singled out fairly quickly. He might even be on Ringold's list. And Kate could be a help winnowing out the chaff on that list. On the other hand, I told myself cynically, maybe it's best to let her go off on her own. I wasn't used to working with a partner and the chances of her turning up anything but bad memories about Twyla were very slim.

It would be a little like sending her out for a left-handed wrench. Not a nice thing to do. But it would keep her busy. And I had the feeling that Kate Davis was never busier or more content than when she thought she was in full command, like that general she was descended from. Not like you, huh? I said to myself. And after thinking that over for a second, I walked back downstairs and out to the car.

The Belton house was a green frame bungalow with a mansard roof and a dormer window set like a hooded eye in the center of its second story. I sat in the Pinto staring at that eye and thinking that I should have been back at the library, culling Ringold's list with Miss Moselle. I should have been doing my job, instead of wet-nursing a green girl detective. But when it came down to it, I didn't have it in me to send Kate Davis on a snipe hunt, even if it was her own idea. It didn't look like fun—going up there and prying her loose from what was probably a sad and embarrassing scene. But the fact was I'd begun to like the girl.

So I got out of the car, walked across the leaf-strewn street and up to the Belton's front door. A short, middle-aged man answered my knock. He had on brown, horn-rim glasses, which were slipping down his nose. And his thick black hair was salted with dandruff, like a sprinkle of fine confetti. He looked like a thousand other men I'd known.

An office-worker, maybe an engineer or a draughtsman—with a face like a fingerprint on an eraser. Eyes all smudged and mouth a dark spot and blue shadows on his cheeks like a day's growth of beard. The only thing that distinguished him from the other bone-weary, middle-management types who put in their forty hours per and come home to drink and to be taken advantage of by their wives and children was the fact that this one had been crying.

I felt hurt for him that he had to be seen like that and suddenly angry at Kate Davis, because that kind of intrusion just wasn't part of anyone's job. He wiped his eyes with a handkerchief and asked who I was in a mellow, grieving voice. And I didn't have a choice but to tell him.

"Come in, then, won't you?" he said politely.

It made me madder that the poor son-of-a-bitch felt he had to be polite, when he should have socked both Kate and me in the jaw for muddying up his life for no good reason.

"Harry!" she said brightly when Belton ushered me into the living room, which was smaller than I'd expected from the look of the house but furnished in the usual eclectic fashion of middle-income homes. A chair or a lamp from every good time or bad since the house was purchased. Furniture like the leaves of a family Bible.

I gave Kate a look and she made a funny expression with her mouth—as if to say, what's bothering you? Then she looked up defiantly from behind her tortoiseshell glasses.

I didn't want to have the row that was going to come in front of poor Belton, who, God knew, had enough heartaches of his own. So I let him seat me on a green, sculpted couch that smelled of tobacco and must and listened politely as he picked it up again—the story of his Twyla.

51

"She didn't have many friends," the man said. "She was never real popular in school. I mean, Jill and I . . ." He swallowed hard. "We pushed her. You know? How parents will push? It's just that we'd seen so much loneliness ourselves as kids. Both of us were younger children from big families, where you don't really get the attention you need. That's why we decided to have only the one. Of course, now . . ."

He sat back on his arm chair, took off his glasses, and began to polish the lenses with his handkerchief, as if he were whetting them on a smooth, round stone.

"She liked to read," he said absently. "She was a great reader of history. It was one of her best subjects—history. History and art. She was going to the art school, you know. Lon Aamons' school. After she'd finished college, she'd gone out and taught for a year. But . . . she didn't like it. Frankly, she wasn't built for teaching. She was too shy and the kids took advantage of her. So, we thought the art thing. You know, commercial art . . ."

Kate said, "Was she going to the school when it happened?"

He nodded. "She'd stay at Lon's place until late on most evenings. And then she had a job painting scenery at the Playhouse. She had some friends, too. Other students. They'd go out for a drink after classes. That night she'd stayed late at the school. We'd thought that she'd gone out to one of the bars in Mt. Adams. I mean that that was why she was so late. It had happened before. So . . . I mean we weren't worried. We'd gone to sleep when they came to the door."

I'd had enough. I got up from the chair and said, "Thank you, Mr. Belton. We won't take up any more of your time." I walked over to Kate and said, "Let's go."

"There may be other questions I'd like to ask you," she said to Belton and gave me a disconcertingly wry look.

The man said, "I'd do anything to find out who killed my daughter." He stared me in the eye and, suddenly, his face quivered as if it were about to fly apart. "Please, mister," he said in a voice that was not quite sane. "Find that terrible bastard. And when you do," he whispered, "kill him."

7

"THAT WAS just swell, Kate," I said to her, as we walked down the sidewalk to the street. "Real good detective work."

She gave me another amused look and said, "Don't you trust your partner, Harry?"

But I was too caught up in my angry mood to hear the laughter in her voice. Mostly because I could see myself, or some inchoate version of me, in Twyla Belton's father. In that breadbox of a house, with the furniture like mismatched plates. And it had scared me.

"You don't go stirring up people's lives without a good reason."

"Oh?" she said mildly. "I thought you did."

I grabbed her by the arm and spun her around. She was only five-feet six, so I had to bend down a little to look in her pretty face, which was sassier than ever beneath its mop of curls. "Why does your nose always look like it's pressed against a window?"

She snorted with laughter. "I've been made love to in nicer ways."

"I'm not making love, Kate. I'm angry."

"If you'd give me a chance, Harry," she said, "I might be able to explain, but we'll have to go back to the library."

"This better be good," I said.

"Or what?" she asked me. "Let's face it. I've got you hooked. Number one, you like the way I look and want to see more of it. Number two, you like the fact that I'm a rookie and make a rookie's mistakes. Number three, my personality prickles you and you see me as a challenge. Should I go on? No, there's no question about it. Sooner or later you're going to fall in love with me, just like Jessie said."

I gawked at her.

"Just being honest, Harry. I decided to be honest with you this morning. Well, last night, really. You see," she said as she turned toward the Pinto, "I'm going to fall in love with you, too."

She got in the passenger side door and said, "Are you coming?"

"I don't know," I said and meant it.

I kept examining her as I drove back to the library to see if she was sprouting a tri-cornered hat and battle ribbons. I've never been much of a determinist. It takes all the fun out of meeting someone for the second time. But by God, that girl was a general's great-grandaughter if I'd ever met one. And I wasn't sure I liked some very tender parts of my life being deployed by such a precise hand.

She liked it. No question about that. Every time she looked over at me, she grinned in a new way. And once she threw her blonde head back and smiled at the roof, as if we were just coming home, drunk and festive, from a New Year's Eve party.

"Lighten up, Kate," I said to her. "People will think I've been beating you."

She laughed. "You're too tense, Harry. You've got a critical parent on your back. I guess that's my fault for laying it on you all at once. I just don't believe in playing games with people I like. When we get back to the library, I'll get you a copy of *Creative Intimacy* and you can do a little research on yourself."

"Are you serious?"

"I don't know? Am I? Greenwald's got a lot of interesting things to say about adult relationships. You know, toxic patterns and toxic individuals?"

"I've had quite a dose of you at this point," I said. "And I don't believe in making love out of a book."

"No?" She put a serious look on her face and said, "That's a critical parent comment, Harry, if I've ever heard one. You're letting old tapes destroy your enjoyment of the present. Did your father ever beat you for reading a book?"

"Keep it up, Kate."

She giggled and said, "We're going to get along, all right. I'll have to whip you into shape. But we're going to get along."

I wonder, I said to myself.

It was four-thirty when we pulled into the library lot. Kate was out of the car before I turned off the ignition. She

56

trotted up the red-brick sidewalk to the big glass-and-chrome doors and glanced back at me over her shoulder before walking inside. It was a lovely look, full of self-deprecating irony and just a touch of real affection, as if she were letting me know that I shouldn't take all of that hokum she'd been spouting—that rare blend of Jessie Moselle's astrology and Eric Berne's transactionalism and her own brand of liberated sexuality—completely seriously. That look made me feel a little saner. Kate Davis's zany brand of lovemaking was affecting, all right. But I was glad to know, or to think I knew, that the brazen manner and T.A. terminology weren't all there was to the real Kate. Of course, you could be wrong, Harry, I told myself. She might be exactly what she seems to be. And what, pray tell, are you going to do with someone like that?

I trudged up the sidewalk after Kate, as if I'd been thoroughly whipped into shape, and found her parking her butt on the circulation desk inside the door. She winked at me as I came in. And I said, "Damn." And wondered again which was the real Kate Davis. What they ought to do, I said to myself, is outlaw a sense of humor among women. And then I asked myself who "they" were and began to think that she was right—that that combination of sass and high seriousness was going to do me in.

"All right, lady," I said. "Where to now?"

"Down, sir," she said and pointed to a stairwell behind the desk. She swiveled around on her butt, gave me another coy look, and hopped off the counter.

"Damn," I said again.

We walked down a spiral staircase to a huge basement storeroom, lined with half-filled bookshelves and lit from above by row upon row of naked bulbs.

"The stacks," she said with a flourish of her hand. "Or the tombs, as we call it around here."

The place smelled strongly of sere paper and of book rot. I ran a finger along one shelf of books and examined the contents. Stodgy, outsized folios, with marbled covers and leather spines. Books without covers, boxed like candy samplers in yellow cardboard containers. Old numbers of defunct magazines and foreign journals. Huge gazeteers and outdated Census reports. A graveyard of wood pulp and printer's ink and all those words, floating through the semi-dark like a faint babble.

"Why," I asked her, "are we here?"

Kate gave me a sexy look and said, "I can think of some interesting answers."

She took my hand and led me up to a dumbwaiter—the kind they used to ship books between floors. Five decrepit volumes were sitting inside. Worn quartos with cracked buckram covers and faint gilded print on the spines.

"Those are five of the books that Twyla Belton withdrew from the library before she was killed. They were brought down here for storage, along with a number of other outdated books. Most of them were given away to charities or sold at book fairs. But for some reason Ringold decided to keep these. Take a look."

I picked up one of the volumes. It was an illustrated edition of Gibbon's *Decline and Fall.* Probably turn-of-the-century, judging by the cover. I opened it up and leafed through the *Life.* There were notes in the margins of the early pages. Little stars and exclamation points and score marks, as if someone had finally found a use for the symbols on the top keys of a typewriter. A few paragraphs had been underlined in faded red ink. And Twyla or somebody had written "Yes!" in big block letters beside several paragraphs. It was typical marginalia, that vehement dialogue we carry on with our books at the top of our voices, as if we were arguing with our grandparents about the new morality. I skipped to the middle of the text, to the glossy section of illustrations, and stopped cold.

She was standing beside me and when I glanced at her face, she nodded slowly, as if she'd come to that same page and had the same reaction. I looked back at the book. It was a photograph of a nude statue of Psyche. "Now in the Louvre in Paris," the citation beneath it read. And someone had taken a razor blade and a ruler to that photo and cut out the statue's breasts and genitals and the unfinished eyes and the mute stone lips.

"Sweet Jesus," I said under my breath. "We really do have a psychopath on our hands."

"Say he found the girl, Twyla, in the library," I said, thinking it out. "Took out the books he'd seen her reading and defaced the illustrations, as if he were practicing on the pictures what he planned to do to the girl herself."

"Maybe the photographs were like fetishes to him," Kate said. "Symbolic representations of Twyla, which he destroyed."

"I don't know about that," I said. "We'll have to talk with a psychiatrist to find out what the photographs may or may not have represented. What I do know is that two years ago, our Ripper tore up some books and then, maybe, tore up a girl. Now he's torn up some more books and I think we better get Ringold's list damn quickly and find out just how many young women have been taking books out of the art section."

"I can do that in the morning," Kate said pertly. "And follow up on it, too. And you can handle the men on the list."

She was dividing things up again, like the impetuous

general's impetuous grandaughter. Deploying the troop. Only this time I didn't mind. Kate Davis had earned her wings as far as I was concerned, and if she wanted to revel in it, that was all right, too.

"You did a good job today," I said to her.

And she grinned triumphantly.

"What would you say to having a drink with me. To celebrate?"

"I'd say yes, Harry." Kate Davis rolled her blue eyes heavenward and said, "It's in the stars."

We went—where else?—to the Bee. Sat in one of the dark cozy booths on the bar level, where we could look out through the glass louvers at the burghers in the dining room or, when we felt like it, exclusively at each other. And as the night got older, we seemed to feel like it more and more often. Hers was not an easy face to dote on. It was, by turns, too ribald and too studiously intent. Like the girl herself it seemed to be split between sass and seriousness, between jokes and a schoolgirl's culture kit. But then she wasn't much more than a schoolgirl in years. And her sense of humor, her impolite refusal to take her own slogans seriously, made even her preachy side seem winning. And, I thought, a little sad, as if she were almost afraid to believe in anything too deeply. When I asked her, very late, with the cocktail piano playing *weltschmerz* and crystal tinkling below us like a metronome, why that should be so, she looked at me with one eye full of laughter and the other full of something like cautiousness.

"Do you think we know each other well enough to be so personal?" she said and only made it sound half a joke.

"You're the stargazer," I said. "You tell me."

60

"And what do I get in return? Do we share intimacies? Is it to that stage, yet? Sharing Intimacies Stage?"

I smiled at her and said, "You're a little drunk."

"I am," she admitted and rolled in her chair. "But that is *de rigueur,* is it not, for the Sharing Intimacies Scene? And what makes you so damn clear-headed, anyway? What makes you so sure I've got intimacies to share?"

"You really want to know?"

"I don't know?" she said. "Do I?"

"You have, Kate, a rare talent for making light of the things you like."

"And you are a pompous chauvinist," she said. "With an overdeveloped superego. And what I suspect is a tender and embarrassed heart. You also have, if I may say so, a very handsome face." She leaned forward tipsily and ran a finger down my cheek.

"I'm going to take you home," I said.

"Whose home?"

"Yours."

"Coward!" Kate cried. "Jessie will be distraught."

"And you will be relieved."

She dropped her finger from my cheek and said, "Why do you say that?" in a hurt voice.

"Because I have the feeling that, in spite of your prognostication, you need more than a day or two to fall in love."

"And what does love have to do with coming home with me?"

"For me?" I said. "Everything. I'm thirty-seven years old, Kate. Well past the one-night-stand period of my life."

She put her tortoiseshell glasses on her nose and peered at me as if I were out of moral focus. "You are terribly

61

old-fashioned and sentimental. You, sir, are a snob."

I plucked her up by the arm and said, "Madam, so are you."

It was only a guess. But then Kate Davis was a dicey lady. And I was betting that under that brass and liberated patter was a young woman capable of hating herself in the morning. And of hating me, too. She certainly didn't act that way at her doorstep on Resor Avenue. Which is where I deposited her around midnight.

"Goodnight, Harry," she said coolly and held out a hand that might have been carved of ice.

I took it and pulled the rest of her to me and kissed her on her full bow of a mouth. It wasn't a passionate kiss. She was too drunk and self-absorbed for that. But it made me feel better. And I think it made her feel a little better, too. Reassured her that she wasn't losing her touch. When she stepped away from my arms, I ran a hand through that coarse mop of golden hair and she purred with content.

"Good night, Kate," I said.

"Harry?" she said as I turned to go. "Jessie *was* right." I turned back to where she was standing and she laughed and said, "Wasn't she?"

8

THE NEXT morning it was Kate Davis who showed up at the library with a big head and a chastened, painted grin on her face. It was nine A.M. and I was sitting at one of the big varnished oak tables with Miss Moselle, sipping coffee from a cardboard cup and listening to a far-fetched but highly entertaining astro-analysis of my character.

"Having been born on the cusp between Scorpio and Sagittarius," she told me, "makes you a difficult man, Harold. You see, Scorpio is a fire sign and Sagittarius is water. And when you combine fire and water . . . " Miss Moselle waved her fingers through the air, to indicate smoke rising from a doused flame. "Steam," she said conclusively.

"Is that bad?" I asked her.

"Oh, heavens, no. Nothing is good or bad in and of itself. A good deal depends upon the house in which you were born." She put a hand to her mouth and whispered, "Some of my colleagues believe that the moment of conception is more determinant of character than the moment of birth. But I don't hold with such salacious nonsense."

"Neither do I," I said.

"Good. Bring me your birth certificate or ascertain the hour and minute of your birth, and I shall make you a chart."

"Done," I said.

And at that moment, Kate Davis came dragging through the door. Jessie took one look and rushed to her aid.

"My dear," she said with concern. "What happened to you?"

"That man," Kate said, pointing a finger at me. "He got me drunk last night, Jess, and . . . "

"And?" Jessie Moselle said with appetite.

"And didn't take advantage of me."

Miss Moselle nodded her head judiciously, as if Kate had just confirmed her diagnosis. "Steam," she said. "Pure steam."

I wasn't sure I liked the way that sounded.

Miss Moselle hurried off on patent-leather pumps to fetch her bottle of stimulant. And Kate wound her way to the table and plopped down beside me. She was wearing denim and lace, Calvin Klein jeans and a frilly blouse that tied at the neck. And she looked, in spite of the hangover, absolutely lovable. All blonde and cream, with just a touch of color on her lips and in the blue of her eyes. I reached across the table and stroked her cheek.

64

"You have, if you don't mind me saying so, a beautiful face."

She snuggled against my hand with a sigh.

"Did I make a fool of myself last night?" she said woefully.

"Your honor is intact."

"That's hardly what I meant. Liquor frees the natural child in me. And it also loosens my tongue. If I said anything . . ."

I smiled at her and said, "All your secrets are still secret."

"I was afraid of that." She propped her chin on her right palm and eyed me glumly. "I think I ought to tell you something. Something I was afraid to say last night." She took a breath and confessed, "I'm not the person I appear to be."

"Oh?"

"No. It's all an act."

"All?" I said.

She grunted. "You're not making this any easier. You said last night that I laughed at the things I loved. There's a reason for that."

"Shall I make a guess?"

"If you insist," she said.

"You were married right out of high school. And after three or four years of growing up and growing apart, you left him. And since then, you've been afraid of hurting someone else the way you hurt him. So you don't get too deeply involved with anyone."

Kate crinkled her nose and blushed deep red. "Am I that transparent?" she said with astonishment.

"Your blue card," I said. "And a little help from Jessie Moselle."

"I see. I should have known I couldn't fool a trained snooper."

"Not when the snooper is scheduled to fall in love with you." I pointed up at the ceiling and said, "The stars. Remember?"

"I remember," she said in a small voice.

I ran a hand through her mop of curls. "You may not know this, yet, Kate. But I'm a grown-up. I can look out for myself."

But I didn't think she believed me. After three or four years of living with a child and then three or four more of feeling guilty for abandoning him, she wasn't going to believe that for awhile. But that was all right. Because I had plenty of time and a real fondness for the brassy girl who was half denim and half lace.

Miss Moselle came back, carrying a tin of aspirin and a cup of water in either hand. Kate smiled at her feebly.

"Take these," Jessie commanded and held out two white buttons.

"And, then, I think we'd better talk to Ringold," I said. "About Twyla Belton and the art books."

"Together?" Kate said, as she swallowed the aspirin.

"We're partners, aren't we?"

"Are we?" she asked dubiously.

"Come on."

I pulled her up by the hand and led her to Ringold's door.

Ringold was hunched over his desk, tormenting a piece of memo paper with a razor-point pen.

"Sit down, Stoner," he said, without looking up.

When he did look up and saw both of us sitting there, his smile settled like the foundations of a house. "Is there something I can do for you, Kate?" he said with heavy policy.

"She's with me," I said.

"This isn't a prom, Stoner," Ringold said, "I'm sure Kate has business to attend to."

"Maybe I'd better go, Harry."

She got to her feet and I jerked her back down beside me.

"Let's get something straight," I said to Ringold. "You hired me, Leon. You didn't buy me. And I'll handle this case as I see fit. If that's not all right with you, then pay me five hundred bucks for two days work and find someone else."

"I'm getting tired of ultimatums, Stoner," he said, straightening up in his chair as people will do when they're trying to discover some backbone.

"You've got an alternative, Leon. Just tell me I'm through."

His lips struggled for the words. But I was confident he wouldn't find them. For one, he wasn't the type to invest a good deal of money in someone and then squander it in a fit of pique. For another, I'd come to him well-recommended and Ringold was a man who lived by reports and recommendations. And finally, he wanted that computer too badly to blow his best chance at earning it.

He recited some of the racier French vowels this time; and his hand went slowly to his brow, like a tin soldier making a mechanical salute. Then he said, "Oh, hell!" Which was probably as profane as he ever got. "Just give me the report."

Kate Davis bit her pretty lip to keep from smiling and I nodded at him, to indicate that we'd settled the matter of provenance once and for all. Then I told him the bad news about Twyla and the books.

67

"Oh, my God," Ringold said. "What are we going to do?"

There wasn't any regulation to cover this one; and for a second, Leon Ringold not only looked like a scared little boy, he acted like one. He wrung his hands, knitted his bland brow and stared helplessly at me, as if he were a kid who'd lost track of his parents at the fair.

"What are we going to do?" he said again.

"Take it easy, Leon," I said to him. "That's what we're here to discuss."

The thought that we'd come to him to fashion policy had a salubrious effect on Leon Ringold. He patted his gray hair as if he were reseating an invisible crown and said, "I suppose we should contact the police," in a businesslike voice. "Yes, that's the first thing we should do. And then I'd better get in touch with the Board and find out how they want to proceed."

"That's swell, Leon," I said. "And in the meantime, Kate and I will try to find a likely suspect."

"And a likely victim," Kate said icily.

Then Ringold came up with the tough one—the one I'd been asking myself. "What if he's not on the list. What if he doesn't belong to the library?"

"That'll make things difficult," I admitted.

"It might help to talk to a clinical psychiatrist," Kate said. "Someone who specializes in . . . "

"Psychopathic killers?" Ringold said dismally.

"Well, criminal psychology. Maybe we could come up with some guidelines."

"I'll look into that this morning," I said. "And I'll also try to make it up to the art school this afternoon, to see if any of Twyla's teachers can remember if she had a special friend, white, male, between twenty and twenty-five years

68

old. And while I'm doing that, Kate and Miss Moselle can narrow down your list."

I turned to Kate and said, "You know what we're after. Any young white males who've taken out art books or the history books or, if we're really lucky, both. And any young girls who might make likely victims."

"And me?" Ringold said.

"Contact Al Foster at the C.P.D. and tell him what we've come up with. And get in touch with the other branches to see if our Ripper has destroyed books anywhere else."

Ringold shuddered. "You don't think there may be other victims, do you?"

"It's a ghastly thought, I agree. But it's got to be checked. Make a list of any books that have been ripped up like ours, and then we'll take a look at the unsolved homicides over the last few years and see if the Ripper has been working outside of Hyde Park."

"He's planning another one, isn't he?" Ringold said. "I mean that's what it looks like, isn't it?"

"That's what it looks like," I said.

9

I CALLED George DeVries at the District Attorney's office and got the name of the consulting psychiatrist employed by the Criminal Court.

"Benson Howell," George told me. "He's got an office on Wellington Place. Why do you want a shrink?"

I told him what we'd uncovered and he got excited again, the way he had on Monday afternoon when I'd first told him about the torn-up books. "Terrific, Harry! Just terrific. I'll talk to Walker and see if I can't get him to reopen the Belton case. We'll even make you a special deputy, Harry boy, if you want to see this thing through."

"I'm not all that crazy about murder investigations,

George. If the D.A.'s office wants to take this on, they're welcome to it."

George said he'd get back to me later in the day. Then I called Howell's office and made an appointment to see him at ten-thirty. The receptionist spoke to me with the sort of saccharine solicitude in her voice that you usually hear from young duty nurses or old mortuary directors. I wasn't quite sure, when I hung up, whether she understood that I was a private detective and not another patient.

I walked out to the circulation desk, gave Kate Davis a peck on the cheek, and told her I was off to Benson Howell's office.

"If he asks you any questions about your childhood, Harry," she called out as I walked to the door, "dummy up or tell him you were an orphan. They don't quite know what to do with that."

Wellington Place is a short, maple-shaded street, lined on the north side with brown-and gray-stone residences that have been converted into offices and on the south by the high, fenced wall of a schoolyard. Some kid was dribbling a basketball behind that wall when I pulled up in front of Howell's brownstone at ten-twenty. Pock-a-pock-a-pock-a. Like the thwack of a hammer against a limber board. It was the only sound on the street, except for the hiss of the wind among the dry leaves. I took a deep breath of cold air and looked around me. It was an idyllic spot for an office, like a big back yard in the suburbs. And the building itself had been nicely restored. Sandblasted to a burnished red and trimmed in a black paint that looked wet to the touch, with tall smoked-glass windows set in the facade and shiny brass fixtures on all the doors and sashes. It could have been a burgher's home. It was that spruce and genial.

A sign hung on a black chain read "Benson Howell, M.D." and beneath it a hand, like the hands you see in the margins of synoptic Bibles, pointed down a walkway to three concrete stairs and a smoked-glass door. I walked down to the door and pressed a lighted buzzer.

"Yes?" a voice called out over an intercom speaker. It was the secretary's voice. I recognized its too-sweet flavor.

"Harry Stoner," I said. "I have an appointment to see Dr. Howell."

The door opened silently, as if it were cushioned by pneumatic springs. I walked through it into a sleek, handsome waiting room, furnished with smart Danish furniture and some very unhappy-looking people.

The spring morning and the sweet voice and silent feet of Dr. Howell's elegant establishment hadn't done much good for the man and the two women who were sitting there, in silence, one on each wall, as if they were bent on keeping their miseries separate and to themselves. I took the fourth wall, beneath a framed lithograph of a blue horse chewing red grass under a black sun, and tried smiling at one of the women—a very fat lady in a sack dress with a blue parrot design. She eyed me with naked curiosity, as if she were asking herself what *my* problem was. I didn't have to guess about hers. Or about that of the frail-looking, blondish man sitting across from me and studying the carpet as if the floor were the proper place for his eyes to rest. The third one, a pretty teenage girl dressed in tight jeans and a halter top that barely held her breasts, was harder to figure out. From the boredom on her face I guessed she was either waiting for someone or that she'd been ordered to come to Dr. Howell by the Juvenile Court. When I looked her way, she tossed her head with a snippy flip and fixed her eyes on the exposed-brick wall across from her chair.

A couple of minutes passed. Very slowly. Then the receptionist, a youngster with lank blonde hair and a country girl's wan, sunken face, came through an opening in the east wall. "Mr. Stoner?" she said.

I got to my feet and the fat lady gave me an ugly look. "Do you think I could speak to the doctor for just a second?" she said in a cranky, indignant voice.

"He's very busy, Mrs. Morris," the girl said automatically.

"It'll only take a second," Mrs. Morris said and her voice got a little panicky.

"I'm sorry. It'll be a few minutes more."

The fat woman slapped her thigh with her palm and pressed her lips together as if she were afraid to utter another word.

As the receptionist and I walked through the portal, I said, "Do you think she'll be all right?"

The blonde girl laughed. "Connie's been coming to the doctor for ten years, Mr. Stoner. Three times a week. And every time she comes, she asks if she can see him for a moment. I think it's her way of letting us know that she's out there."

The girl led me down a hallway to a big oak door. "Just go in," she said. "He's expecting you."

I walked into Howell's office. It was glassed-in on the north and west walls and paneled in redwood on the south and east. Howell was seated in a leather chair, gazing out the north window at the maple trees that fell away down a hillside behind the office building. From the doorway all I could see of him was the top of his head, which was thick with kinky brown hair, save for a little white baldspot the size of a silver dollar at the crown.

"Come in, Mr. Stoner," he said in a lively, high-pitched

voice. "George DeVries told me you were going to stop by."

He turned in his chair and I got my first look at his face. His thick brown hair was combed back from the forehead in an old-fashioned pompadour that made his head look as square as a picture frame. His features were coarse—nose like the bill of a toucan, green eyes set so closely together they looked crossed, skin lumpy with acne scars. He wore thick gold-rim glasses, a tiny black bow tie, and a tweed suit. All in all, he looked like a small, neat, nervous George S. Kaufman.

Benson Howell looked me over, frowned, smiled, then switched his gaze to a bookshelf built into the paneling on the east wall. He kept right on frowning, smiling, and looking away for the half hour or so that we talked. I got the impression that that was his way of showing off; for Benson Howell was a prima dona, and the little tics and nervous glances weren't involuntary. They were deliberate assertions of his powers of mind, as if he'd never yet found a subject enormous enough to engage his full attention. I didn't know how that act worked on patients like Mrs. Morris. Maybe it gave them a sense of confidence to know that their analyst was so blithe and prepossessed. It certainly put *me* off. I found that I had to make myself concentrate on what he was saying rather than on the arrogant blur of his face, or I think I might have gotten up and left.

As it turned out, it was a good thing I stayed, because the son-of-a-bitch was just as bright as he thought he was and a regular mine of useful information.

I told him about the Ripper, about Twyla and the books, about what Sachs had seen, and about what we had concluded.

Howell raised a caterpillar eyebrow when I finished,

tapped his front teeth with a nicotine-stained forefinger, and said, "You know I'm primarily a forensic psychiatrist. This practice is just a way of keeping myself busy when I'm not in court." His eyes darted about the room and came to rest on a bronze bust of Freud. He curled his lip a bit and said, "What I mean to say is that I'm generally consulted about criminal matters *after* the fact of the crime. And I'm usually given the chance to interview the criminal." He looked up from Freud and out the north window at the maple trees. "It's really an extraordinary challenge," he said without the slightest enthusiasm, "to try to analyze a psychopath without actually examining him." He finally looked at me. "I think that's what you're asking for, isn't it? An analysis of how this man's mind might work? A profile that would help you identify him?"

I said, "Yes. And in layman's terms, Doctor, if you please."

"Extraordinary," he said again, tapped his eye-tooth and looked down at the creamy carpeting. "Extremes, Mr. Stoner. That would be your first clue. Be on the lookout for a man of extremes. Extremes in dress, in look, in occupation, in temperament. Especially in temperament." He looked up and said, "Are you planning to interview your suspects or just to keep them under surveillance?"

"Interview them, if possible," I said.

Benson Howell got to his feet, walked over to the bookshelf and ran his finger along a row of blue, paper-covered periodicals. "Ask him what he would do in a fight."

"In a fight?" I said. "You mean in a fist fight?"

"Yes, in a fight. The man you want won't have any respect for his own body. He will be capable of tremendous violence without apparent fear of injury. He will talk of fighting as if his body didn't exist, the way young children sometimes act when they throw themselves off roof-tops in imitation of Superman. He will talk as if he were all-powerful and invulnerable. Extremes, you see."

"How would he behave in a real fight?"

"Just as he speaks," Benson Howell said. "As if he were invulnerable. Are you planning to do any research on your suspects?"

"Of course," I said. "I'll work up case histories on each one. Or, at least, on the promising ones."

"Then let me give you a typical history. A profile of what your man is like. Understand, there may be individual differences. But, in the main, your Ripper's personality should fit this description." He walked back to his chair, flicked a spot of ash off the cushion, and sat down again. "To begin, he will undoubtedly come from a broken home. He may have been abused as a child. Perhaps by a sadistic father or an overweening, brutal mother. He will most certainly have a marked ambivalence toward his family, and it will extend into every aspect of his emotional life. His sexual experiences will have been short-lived and unsatisfactory. His own sense of sexual identity is likely to be diffuse. He may, in fact, have had homosexual experiences, although he wouldn't recognize them as such. At this point in his life, he is a loner, incapable of sustaining a relationship with anyone outside the love-hate relationship he's formed with his parents and siblings. You will probably discover that he has a history of violent behavior. And if he doesn't," Howell said, "his schoolmates and his teachers—look especially to his teachers and counselors in high school—will remember him as giving the impression of violence, as if human sympathy were dead inside him from the start. He may be working at a distasteful job. As a gravedigger, say, or a garbage man. Or he may have no job at all. And this is important: he is likely to be a religious fanatic. Extremes, again. A man of this type, with his strong ambivalence toward authority figures, has no internal checks on his behavior. No conscience, as we call it. Instead he depends on God, or what he imagines to be God, to regulate his actions personally. It is a grandiose delusion. But your Ripper will share with a narcissist the idea that he is at the center of the universe. One of God's elect. And he will try to act that role. Since sexual feelings are incompatible with such a delusion, he will tend to project his libido onto the women who excite him. In this way, they seem to be the libidinous ones, the evil-doers. And thus, your Ripper maintains his purity and strength."

"How might he have acquired these delusions?"

"From his parents," Howell said. "Especially if he had a father or mother who was held up to him as a model of perfection. And whom he tried to emulate—unsuccessfully. You have to remember, Mr. Stoner, that you'll be dealing with one of life's losers. A man who has failed at everything he's ever tried. All he has going for him are his delusions of grandeur. And he will fight with incredible fury to keep them intact. It goes without saying that this man is likely to be clever. He would have to be clever in order to shore up his defenses in the face of overwhelming realities. He may also be quite charming and intelligent."

Howell tapped his teeth and said, "I have known several charming killers."

"I don't suppose you could help me with a physical description?" I said.

"Yes, I think I might," he said suavely. "He is most likely to be a man of average to below-average size. Not large, like yourself, Mr. Stoner. Large men generally give an impression of power without having to assert themselves. They need not act violently to prove their strength. He may also be tattooed. There is a marked tendency among psychopathic individuals to have themsélves tatooed. And, of course, the nature of the tattoo is a key to the nature of the psychosis. It may sound old-hat, but if your man has good and evil or the like tatooed on opposite arms, be *very* careful, indeed. Since he has repressed almost all of his aggressive feelings, he is more likely to be a quiet individual than a talkative one. He is saving his anger up, you see, for one violent act. You might also look at his pupils. The narrower they are, the greater the rage he's suppressing."

Howell stared off into space again. And I took a deep breath. His casual way of delivering the brutal truth had unsettled me a little. And then it's always chilling to hear what can happen to a human mind, a mind like your own.

I took another deep breath and said, "Do you think he'll try again? Do you think he'll kill a second time?"

"Oh, most certainly," Benson Howell said. "Unless his life has miraculously turned about, he will have built up an incredible rage over two years. Enormous, Mr. Stoner. Like the power of suns. Well, imagine trying to suppress your sexual instincts for two years. Then add to that the grossest indignities that loneliness, guilt, fear, and impotence can cost a man. Oh, yes, Mr. Stoner, he'll try again with all his might. He'll select another victim as he did the first time— for some vague resemblance she might bear to his mother or to a sister or to some girlfriend, real or imagined. Or he may choose her for the simple reason that she excites him greatly and, therefore, terrifies and infuriates him greatly. He will try to repress his desire and when he fails, he'll project his own sexual longing onto his victim. That may be the moment when he begins to cut up the pictures. Or he may do that for a period of time before the transference occurs. Working off steam, as it were, before blowing up. But he *will* blow up. And when he attacks, he will feel as if God Himself is propelling him onward, as if he is cutting out evil—not human flesh. He'll kill again, unless you stop him. But understand what you're up against. This man has no realistic fear of injury. He is filled with murderous rage and with an indignant sense of his own injured righteousness. He will be clever, ruthless, and as merciless as God meting out punishment to sinners."

"And there's no way to shut him down?" I said. "No way short of violence."

"That depends on the situation, of course," Howell said. "He does have an Achilles heel. The very source of his power—his grandiose delusions—can be his worst weakness. You see, he hungers for the acclamation that life has denied him. He lives for notoriety. If you catch him off-guard or simply at the right moment, he may confess on the spot. They love to confess their powers. It is, in fact, the reason why they send notes and leave clues for the police. Indeed, those pictures he's cut up are just such a clue. A warning, if you will. Or a cry for help. You see most psychopaths want to be caught."

"Let's hope the Ripper is one of them," I said.

10

I WALKED back through Benson Howell's office up those three stone steps into a blue noon, full of sunlight, and stood where I had stood an hour before, looking out across Wellington at the high stone wall of the schoolyard. I listened for the sound of the basketball. But the kid had gone in. Even the wind had died down. And it was as still and listless as a high summer day along the street. Which no longer seemed so genial to me, so placid and suburban. Not after my encounter with the doctor.

I found the Pinto parked in a bed of maple leaves, cracked open the door, jabbed my key into the ignition and flipped on the radio to a local talk show. I needed to hear some mindless chatter, just to wash the sound of Howell's voice out of my head and, I guess, to sober me up.

I once heard a psychiatrist say that when we lie down to sleep, we're lying down beside a horse and an alligator, beside an old mammalian brain and an even older reptilian one, to go along with our modern cerebral cortex. Well, there's enough reptile sleeping inside me to recognize the real thing when I come across it. And I'd just heard a description of a brute who made my blood run cold. Of course, shock was Howell's game. Maybe because he was used to speaking from a witness stand, where subtlety pays no dividend. But even taking his manner into account, I was left with one very dangerous psychopath. And at that moment, I didn't feel like facing up to the responsibility.

So I listened to the radio, to a gravel-voiced man who was passing out advice to the lovelorn with the easy hand of a back-yard gossip, and told myself that there was a good chance that the District Attorney's office would take the Hyde Park Ripper off my back. I even flirted with the notion of calling DeVries from a booth at the top of the street— to find out whether he'd talked his boss, Walker Parsons, into reopening the Belton case. But George had only had an hour to work, and it would take a morning at least to get Walker Parsons interested, *if* he got interested at all. Which was not the sure thing I wanted to believe it was.

Like Leon Ringold, Parsons was essentially a book-keeper, a ledger-man with a shrewd sense of his own limitations. He was not a very bright man and he knew it. He wasn't even a good lawyer. What he was was a mediocre politician with a knack for making his own mediocrity palatable. Walker had a schoolboy's notion of good and a Baptist's notion of evil, and for better than ten years he'd ridden through administration changes and police scandals on the back of a simple wish—to make things better for the decent folks. The decent folks understood and kept right on electing him. They knew they'd have to go a long way to find a man as safely innocent of thought as Walker Parsons.

Under normal circumstances, a psychopathic killer would be certain to get Walker's juices flowing. A sure-fire headline and a sure-fire conviction were the sorts of things that registered in his head like dollar signs in a thought balloon. Only this wasn't a sure-fire case—not like the smut-peddling cases that were his forte. And Parsons had already spent a good deal of the taxpayer's money on Twyla's killer two years before. He might just sit back and wait for the Ripper to strike again, wait for the newspaper headlines to build, before going before the grand jury. I made it a fifty-fifty proposition, which meant that there was an even chance that I'd still be on the case at the end of the day.

Not a pretty prospect, Harry. But neither was another homicide on what I'd begun to think of rather fondly as my own turf. And then there was that girl.

So get going, brother, I said to myself. Slip the Pinto into gear and drive over to East Walnut Hills, to Lon Aamons' art school, and start earning your pay. Start acting like a detective instead of like a scared little boy.

And the scared little boy said, "Ha!"

Lon Aamons was a tall, silver-haired old man with a tanned, weathered face as gnarled and fleshless as nut meat. He dressed like a westerner in a plain white shirt, bolla tie, peg-leg slacks and glossy rattlesnake boots. And he spoke with the dry good humor of a man who's used to talking before an audience—a storyteller's slow, flat drawl.

82

He had the look of a good storyteller, flint-eyed and acerb and as spare as bone. The paneled study in which we were sitting was decked with western art and artifacts. Navajo rugs, a collection of Kachina dolls in a huge glass breakfront, silver bracelets flecked with turquoise in a small case and, on the walls, paintings of cowboy scenes done in the romantic style of Remington. It was a man's man of a study, right down to the brace of pistols in a presentation box on his desk and the smells of stale cigar smoke and old leather in the air. But as I sat there listening to him talk, I began to catch the other smells, like the odor of another life, lived down the hall in the big open-air studios where Aamons held classes. The chalky smell of oil paints and of the tarry-black inks they used on the offset presses. Turpentine smell, acrid as fresh onion. And the strong scent of the etching acids. I also got a happy sense of what it was like to be a student in one of those studios, in a school that was like a big, stone ranch house, run by a humorous old man sitting behind his desk in a room filled with his own paintings and with antiques set out like stick candy in big glass jars.

"It's not a first-class school," Lon Aamons admitted to me and managed to sound almost proud. "But I wasn't a first-class artist." He pointed with a cigar stub at the sentimental pictures on the walls. "Those are all tall tales. But then most art is like a lie." He put his chin on his hand and said, "Don't tell nobody I said that."

I told him I wouldn't.

"You being a detective," he said, "I thought I'd better get your word of honor. Don't want people saying that Lon talks down the art business. It'll kill my trade. What brings you here, anyway? One of my kids get in trouble?"

"Two years ago," I said. "Her name was Twyla Belton."

Aamons dropped one hand to his desk and sat back heavily in his armchair. He wasn't the kind of man who showed his feelings readily. That would be bad manners, like using your knife to eat peas. Instead, he teased them out like narratives, in the sour disappointed voice of the born storyteller. Only Twyla's name got to him, right through the crust, and made him squint and pull at the cigar stub as if it were a plug. "They find out who did it, did they?" he said after a moment.

"No. That's what I'm working on now."

"Her parents hire you?"

I shook my head. "I have reason to believe that the boy who killed Twyla may be planning to kill another girl."

"Dear God," Lon Aamons said softly and sat upright in his chair. "How can I help?"

"Well, if she had a boyfriend that would help."

"I went through that with the police," he said with mild disappointment, as if he were hoping I'd have something more specific to ask of him. He really did want to help. And suddenly I knew exactly how a man with a painter's eye for detail could help me.

"Tell me about her, then. Tell me what she was like."

"You could get that better from her parents."

"Not better," I said. "Just more sentimentalized. I need a clear-eyed portrait of Twyla Belton. Because something about her, something about the way she looked or talked or acted, set this madman off. I'm betting that same something is setting him off again. So tell me about her, Mr. Aamons. And in your own words."

He wiped at his upper lip. "I want to say one thing before we get into this. I liked that girl. And if there's a question of money involved in this . . ." He looked away as if the word itself embarrassed him. "I mean if you need funds to help corner this son-of-a-bitch . . ."

I told him that money wasn't a problem.

"Then I guess I can do as good a job as anybody telling you about Twyla. 'Cause she was a good one, and I don't see a lot of her kind of talent around here. Most of my kids come by way of junior colleges or straight out of high school. They just don't have the skills or the time for a career in fine arts. Some of them don't have any skill, at all. Just a longing to be special. Lord, it's a bitter disappointment to learn that a broken heart don't buy you a thing in this world. A lot of them can't take that lesson and give up on the spot. Spend the rest of their lives nursing a grudge and telling themselves that someday they'll paint their pictures and put the record straight. Art's a paltry enough thing as it is. But, my gosh, it makes a lousy excuse. More would-be human beings running around pretending to be would-be artists than you could count on both hands and feet. Not her, though. She had half the equipment it takes to make a good artist. She had all the talent in the world."

"And the other half?" I said.

Aamons touched his stomach and frowned. "She didn't have the guts. She didn't have the heart. Why, hell, she wouldn't have been at the school at all if she'd had what it really takes to get on." He laughed bitterly. "You see, she wasn't very pretty. At least, not the kind of pretty she wanted to be. And, man, that can hurt when you're young. Had a sweet round face, like a child's drawing of mother. All cheerful circles, from forehead to chin. And then she was as pudgy as a baby's hand. And just as eager as hell to please. Which made her fair game for just about every snot-nosed bully in the joint."

85

He got up from his chair and walked over to a closet set in the paneled wall. "Should have thought of this earlier," he said. "It's just been so many years."

He dug into the closet and fished out a black portfolio.

"This is some of her work," he said, wiping the portfolio gently with his right hand. "I haven't looked at it since she died. But if you want to know what kind of girl she was, what and who she liked, just look in here, and let her tell you."

Aamons set the portfolio on the desk in front of me and untied the string fastener. "She was going to be a wildlife illustrator," he said. "At least, that's what she was aiming at. Take a look at these."

He opened the portfolio to a watercolor sketch of feeding giraffes. "She did a whole series of these at the zoo. All sorts of animals. Even when she was drawing people, she was thinking animals, as if the world were a kind of beast-fable to her, as if that were her way of taming it."

I stared at the drawing, which was, in fact, exquisitely done. Softened and not just by the medium. Colors blurred but outlines uncannily true-to-life, as if the colors were floating inside the animals or inside her, like vague powers of mind or of mood.

Aamons flipped the page to a drawing of two lions, sitting the way competitive dogs sit, in a T—the dominant one at the top. The tawny colors that floated through them and around them had a wild kind of beauty, as if the colors themselves were on the prowl.

"Can you imagine this sort of thing in the *Geographic* or in *Wild Life?*" he said with a fierce pride. "She was too damn original for them. She had her own way of seeing things and, if you look close enough, it wasn't a bit sentimental. Not a bit like my own poor stuff. She didn't look like any-

86

body else, taming her beasts that didn't want to be tamed. You see, it's almost like she's incorporated the way we look at them, the animals in a zoo, into the animals themselves. As if they were aware of us watching them and didn't much give a damn. None of that monkey behind the bars malarkey."

He flipped through pages of tigers, deer, antelope. All of them little allegories of perceiver and perceived, of what's wild in us and what's severe and undefinable in them. Then he came to a series of line drawings done in a more realistic, less interesting style.

"Some of her early stuff," he said.

I recognized sketches of Eden Park, the Conservatory, Seasongood Pavillion, and one chilling one of the Overlook, where she'd been killed. I stared at it and Aamons sighed.

"They'd all go up there to draw. It's such a damn pretty place. But she wasn't taken in by mere pretty even then. Not in her drawings she wasn't. Look what she picked to center on."

It was the famous bronze statue of Romulus and Remus being suckled by a wolf, given to the city by some citizens of Rome in honor of the fact that Cincinnati, too, was built on seven green hills above a river. The pretty part was there, in the background. The blue, leaf-strewn ponds. The low stone wall looking out on the Ohio. The Japanese bridge that arcs over the reflecting pool. But it was all thrown out of kilter by the statue, which, like the moody coloring of her animals, seemed to float through the sketch like a theme, as if this, too, were another beast fable.

"The rest is miscellaneous stuff," Aamons said. "Snapshots. Figure studies. Things that caught her eye."

He showed me line drawings of arms, hands, legs. No

faces. Then he turned to one that made my blood run cold.

"Hold it!" I said and slapped my hand on the page.

Aamons looked startled. "What?" he said nervously.

For a moment I couldn't say anything. I didn't have the breath. It's just a forearm, Harry, I said to myself. Just a man's forearm. Propped, it seemed, on a table top beside an open book. Probably on one of the library table tops on the second floor where she'd been sketching one fall afternoon two years before. And, of course, what had caught her eye, that fine eye attuned to the wild and the tame, was what was pictured on the arm. It was what had stopped me, too, and sent me hurtling back one hour in time, to Benson Howell's sanitized office. On the forearm, just as Howell'd said there might be, was a tattoo of a fanged cobra, twisted murderously about a woman's naked body, with the slogan "Evil" printed beneath it, as if it were an emblem in an emblem book. It was almost too good to be true.

"My God," I said.

And Aamons said, "For crying out loud, what's going on?"

I looked up at him. "This could be him. This could be the Ripper."

He looked bewildered. "You mean the man who killed Twyla?"

I nodded. "She couldn't have known it," I said, half to myself, in a voice that was probably as stunned sounding as Aamons' own. Then I started to get excited. The detective in me took over and began looking ahead, planning it out. "I'll need this drawing, Mr. Aamons."

"Sure," he said.

"I'll get the police to make copies of it and we'll see if they've got anyone on file with this tattoo on his arm. Then I can check the people on the list."

"What list?" he said in confusion. "What are you talking about?"

"It's too complicated to explain. Let's just say that you've probably given me the next best thing to a photograph of Twyla's killer. And I'm going to nail him with it before he gets the chance to cut up anyone else."

"I did that?" he said with pleasure.

"You and Twyla," I said. "She didn't know it, but she drew his picture for us. Probably in the very place where he'd first seen her and first thought of killing her."

"Son-of-a-bitch," Lon Aamons said. "What a piece of justice."

I took a deep, satisfied breath and said, "Yeah."

11

IT WAS close to one o'clock when I nosed onto the expressway at Taft and headed down the Mt. Adams hillside, past
the Baldwin warehouse, to town. An hour or so before, I'd
been ready to quit the case or to turn it over to the D.A.'s
staff. Now I felt as if there weren't enough hours left in the
day to do the job I had to do. And not just *had* to do, but
wanted to do. After hearing about the girl, after hearing the
affection in that old man's voice and seeing the touching
legacy she'd left behind her, some part of me, almost as old
and hardbitten as the Ripper himself, was determined that
there weren't going to be any more Twyla Beltons on this
case. No more sacrifices to someone's stunted sense of his

90

own importance. Because once you'd demystified him, once you'd gotten over the thrill of horror that freezes you when you come in contact with someone terrible, you see what he's left behind him for what it is—the savaged books and the torn-up girl and those sad, sensitive drawings. And weighing them all in the same balance, you start to see that the Ripper, or anyone like him, just doesn't deserve the tribute that a slightly crazy man always pays a truly crazy one. He'd gotten his measure of pity and fear out of me. Now it was the girl's turn.

I had two stops to make before returning to the library and the first was simple enough. I got off Reading at Central Parkway, drove north through the blue afternoon haze to Station X, parked in the Music Hall lot, and with the sketch tucked under my arm, walked across Ezzard Charles to the police building and Al Foster's tiny office.

He lit a fresh cigarette when I showed him the sketch and almost cracked a smile.

"I knew I could count on that heart of yours, Harry," he said. He tapped the drawing with his forefinger. "You sure that's him?"

"It would be a pretty weird coincidence if it wasn't. The tattoo fits the description I got from the court psychiatrist, and the drawing was made about the time of the murder. I figure she must have spotted him in the library. What happened after that is speculation."

"You'd make a great witness," Al said.

I laughed. "Then try this out. She was a romantic girl with more imagination than experience. When you add loneliness to that combination and a native sympathy for wild animals, you might get someone who would go up to the Overlook with a slightly off-beat stranger, who had a tattoo on his arm like a badge of his own wild nature."

91

"All right," he said. "I don't know about the scenario. Maybe he just followed her up there. Maybe there wasn't any contact between them at all—I mean, beyond the drawing and the murder itself. That doesn't matter. If this is him, *I* want him. And I don't care if DeVries and the D.A.'s office goes for it or not." Foster crushed out a smouldering butt with his thumb and said, "I saw that kid's body, Harry. And I'm telling you I want this guy. So I'm going to run this sketch for you. This afternoon. And if we come up with anybody on file with this sort of tattoo on his arm, I'll let you know as soon as possible. You'll be at the library?"

I said, yes.

"One thing, though," Foster said. "If we do get a make on this guy, *don't* go handling it on your own. You can case him, all right. I'll even deputize you. But when it comes time for a bust, you call me. Understand? If worse comes to worst, I can get a John Doe warrant and pull him in for vagrancy."

"I'm no hero, Al," I said.

He didn't say anything.

I drove across town to the Court House, which was stop two, and found George DeVries staring out the window again in his second-floor office.

"They really keep you busy, don't they, George?" I said from the doorway.

He turned slowly around in his chair. I could see from the disappointed look on his face that he'd already had his little talk with Walker Parsons and that it hadn't gone the way he'd wanted it to. He tried to explain it to me, in that sour, mechanical tone of voice that hired hands generally adopt when they don't see eye-to-eye with their bosses.

"Wally's got an election coming up," he said and bit his

lip. "He thinks the timing's wrong on this thing, and he wants to wait until the end of the month to break it to the papers. You see he's got a close one this time, what with the boy Jackson giving him such a hard time in the second district. And this kind of case could send him right over the top. If the timing's right." He made an embarrassed face and sat back in his chair. "I'm sorry as hell, Harry. He's willing to make you a special deputy, if that's any consolation. And if you had a name, he says it might be different.

"Aw, hell," George said. "Let's face it. Walker hasn't got the guts of an egg-suck dog. If he did, he wouldn't be prosecuting the porno-peddlers all the time and letting the really big-time crooks go scot free. But he *does* know how to get himself reelected. And come October, that's all he's got on his mind. I'm sorry, Harry, but there's not a thing I can do on my own."

I told him not to worry about it—that I might have a name for him in a couple of days.

"Yeah?" he said eagerly. "That could make a difference."

Only I wasn't so sure. Walker was perfectly capable of sitting on an indictment for a month and letting the Hyde Park Ripper wander around the streets until he needed him to cash in at the polls. As I walked back down the stairway to the lobby, I decided to stick with Al Foster and the P.D., if I did make my man. They would get him off the streets, all right. Maybe permanently, Harry, I said to myself. And wasn't so sure I cared about that, either.

I'd run my errands and it was time to return home. Past time, really. It was almost three-thirty by my watch. Which meant that Kate Davis was probably wondering if I'd decided to renege on our partnership again. She didn't have a slow fuse, Kate. Or a constant faith in male detectives with ingrown parental tapes or whatever-the-hell it was I was supposed to be suffering from. She might just have taken it upon herself to investigate that list on her own. Not a good idea, if she happened on the right name. What I should have done, I thought, was call. And then I laughed at myself for turning so domestic on the basis of a single kiss. Only when I started thinking about that kiss and about her pert face and lush figure and that mop of curls that felt like crushed velvet to the touch, I began to wonder why I'd stopped at one.

Ingrown parental tapes, Harry? Or just a bit of old-fashioned anxiety. A touch of fear before the plunge. Before committing yourself one more time, steadfast as the good soldier, to love. The enormous exercise of love. The obligation, the duty of love. Fairly pleasant duty, though. I thought again about Kate Davis's pretty, sportive face, about the slender curve of her neck and the swell of her breasts, and pushed down on the accelerator.

She was a little peeved, all right, when I walked through the library doors at four. But when I told her all I'd learned about Twyla and the Ripper, patiently and in complete detail so she'd get the point that I was still her faithful partner, she seemed pleased. She seemed pleased with the way I was looking at her, too. Pleased and a little flustered, like a teenage girl before her first date. That afternoon, as we sat across from one another at one of the varnished oak library tables, was a fresh start. And both of us knew what we were starting. She ducked her head and straightened her glasses on her nose and grinned at me, with her hand to her forehead and those blue eyes wide with excitement. And I grinned back at her with the sort of wonder that I always feel when I realize that the girl sitting across from me, the girl with whom I'm about to share not only a bed but a history—a portion of my life and my past—has a life and a past of her own. I imagine that people who have lived together for decades must feel it, too. Must look up, now and then, and see a stranger sitting across from them—another person who will never quite fit the history that the two of them have created together. I suppose if you ever lose that sense of mystery—because that's what it is, folks—the relationship dies. I didn't know how long she'd stay interested in me, but I had the feeling that even a detective could spend a long while finding Kate Davis out.

I think we might have held hands across the tabletop, if Ringold hadn't ambled up with his famous list.

"Here it is," he said, eyeing us suspiciously. "Kate and Jessie have culled it thoroughly and they've come up with four possible male suspects and six female . . . what shall I say? Victims?" He slapped the list on the table between us like a gavel. "I did what you asked and called the police. I've also contacted the other branches about the possible mutilation of their art books. Now what have you got to report to me?"

"Good news," I said. "I think we've got a description of the Ripper."

I thought he might swoon. He rocked on his heels and his eyes got very large; then he broke into a big, sheepish grin.

"That is good news," he said with genuine cheer. "My gosh, how did you do it?"

"A little detective work," I said and winked at Kate. "And some very good luck. Twyla Belton was not only an art student, she was a very good artist. And she may have left one sketch of the Ripper behind her."

"What does he look like?" he said curiously.

95

"I don't know."

Ringold made a confused face, as if he weren't quite sure I wasn't twitting him again.

"What I've got, Leon," I said. "Is a sketch of a tattoo on the Ripper's forearm. But if it is him, it's distinctive enough to be used to make a positive I.D. All we have to do is find which one of the four people on our list has that tattoo on his arm and we'll have our killer."

"Wonderful!" Ringold said and clapped his hands. Then he looked confused again. "What if he's not on our list?"

"According to Dr. Howell, the man we want is likely to have a history of violent behavior. I've already contacted Al Foster at Central Station, and he's going to run our description through C.I.D. They'll cross-check their records and come up with a tidy list of felons who have this kind of tattoo on their forearms. There won't be a lot of them I guarantee you, because it's a distinctive design."

"Spare me," Ringold said.

He turned to go, whirled back around on his heels, cleared his throat, pinched the knot in his tie as if it were a tiny microphone, and said, "You've done a very good job." He nodded to Kate and added, "Both of you."

He walked briskly away, back to his office, leaving Kate staring after him with her mouth ajar.

"You'll catch flies," I said to her.

She shook her head and said, "I just never expected to hear that." She beamed at me. "Thanks. I'll pay you back sometime."

"How 'bout tonight?"

She pulled at her frilly white blouse and said, "How 'bout right now?"

I grinned at her. "Woman, you keep surprising me."

"You're still too hung up, Harry," she said with grave

authority. "You're not impetuous enough. You're not allowing your natural child to have a good time."

I shook my head and she laughed.

"Tonight will be fine," Kate Davis said.

We went through the list name by name, Kate, Miss Moselle and I. Sitting about the little desk behind the circulation counter. With Miss Moselle's box of index cards at her side. The application forms didn't really tell us much more than names, addresses, and birthdates. But Miss Moselle had "a little something," as she put it, on most of the library's patrons. Who took what from where. Who was habitually late returning books. Who was belligerent with the librarians. Who was rowdy in the stacks. What each one looked like and what the stars, the imperishable, whirling stars, told her about their characters.

"To begin with, no tattoos," she said. "I would certainly remember a tattoo. Ugly things, they affect me like the smell of a cheap cigar left smoldering in an ashtray. I have a physical revulsion to them."

"That isn't so good, Jess," Kate said unhappily.

"On the other hand," Miss Moselle said. "I cannot be certain that I have seen the forearms of each of these boys. I try not to look at the forearms of young men. I have a slightly different reaction to them. But no less marked."

Kate and I laughed.

Jessie Moselle blushed bright red and Kate patted her gently on the hand.

"I have the same reaction," she said.

Miss Moselle drew herself up in the chair. "Shall we take these names alphabetically?" she said with great dignity.

I nodded.

"Then we shall begin with Gerald Arnold. A fine old

97

English name, Arnold. He is a Scorpio, which makes him mercurial," she said, glancing at me. "He is, as I recall, of medium height. Quite slender. With very long blonde hair and rather a ragged beard. He often wore peace emblems and religious symbols on his clothes and about his neck."

"A born-again hippie?" I said.

"Oh, I wouldn't know about that," she said, as if being a Jesus-freak to Miss Moselle were equivalent to membership in some secret society, like the Masons. "He did dress in denim clothing and was often in need of a bath. But I don't think labels like 'hippie' are of much use, do you? Some of my favorite patrons have long hair. Indeed, it wasn't until the last century that short hair became fashionable. It was a Prussian fad, you know. Odious people, the Prussians. I'm sure they thought short hair would be more convenient in warfare."

"And the next one?" I said. "Haskell Lord?"

"A Capricorn. Which is a very perplexing sign. Half-goat and half-fish, you see. One part pointing downward and the other pointing up. This could be one worth looking into, I think, depending on what house he was born into. Besides, I remember him as being a very disagreeable young man. Dark-haired, swarthy, muscular. With rather a rude manner. I must admit that I haven't seen him about in many months. But he could be sulking. He failed to return his last withdrawal of books and we had to threaten to revoke his card in order to get them back. I believe his brother or his mother finally brought them in."

"And Isaac Mill?"

"A Cancer. A moon sign. He could easily be as mad as a hatter. Which is a peculiar phrase. It comes from the fact, I believe, that hatters used fulminate of mercury to work their felts and the vapors often made them giddy and contentious. Rather like our modern glue-sniffers. I may be being a bit hard on Mr. Mill, as he was a very quiet fellow. Very neat and well-groomed and polite. But he had a little toothbrush moustache, like Hitler's. And I'm afraid it made me hate him. Oddly enough, we had to threaten him with a final notice, too. He claimed he'd been out of town and hadn't received our first and second notices. I tend to believe it, but I may be leaning too far toward charity since I secretly despised him."

"And finally Lester Towne."

"A Sagittarian," she said with delight. "Sign of philosophers and poets. Although we can be rather impractical, as well. Lester, I'm afraid, is a bit on the impractical side. Quite odd, really, and terribly forgetful. He left his umbrella in the periodical reading room no less than three times last year. And he doesn't seem to be able to hold onto anything else. His mother, who comes here often, tells me that he's lost his job, too."

"Which was?" I said.

"He worked for the coroner's office, I think. Driving an ambulance."

I felt like laughing when Miss Moselle had finished and departed upstairs to help her plump friend at the juvenile desk.

"She could have made it easier," I said to Kate. "Each one of them has one or two of Howell's identifying features. If I didn't know Miss Moselle better, I'd say she'd done it on purpose."

"I guess that's the problem," Kate said, "when you start comparing people to a pathological model. We all end up looking a little mad."

"Fine words, coming from you."

"Don't be critical, Harry," she said tartly.

"All right," I said. "What about your six girls?"

"I've already been through the list with Jessie. Of course, that was before you'd talked to Mr. Aamons. What do you think I should be looking for?"

I shook my head wearily. "I'm not sure. According to Benson Howell it could have been a purely physical thing. The Ripper's version of lust. Or Twyla may have resembled someone in the Ripper's family or one of his friends."

"Then I'll need a photograph of her."

"On the other hand, it could have been something about her manner. Some characteristic gesture or look or something about her voice. Our Twyla was a romantic girl, we know that much. And she was lonely. And she did not think of herself as attractive. The murder at the Overlook could have been the upshot of a rendezvous she'd made with our friend."

"That would be pretty unsophisticated, wouldn't it?" Kate said. "Going off to the park with a sullen boy with a serpent on his arm whom she'd probably met in a bar?"

"Unsophisticated and pretty daring," I said. "Her drawings suggest that she was attracted to wild animals. Maybe she was intrigued with this fellow. Or maybe she felt sorry for him. Or it could be that she was just a very lonely girl looking for a little excitement."

"I sincerely hope that I'm never that lonely," Kate said.

"I'll see to it," I told her.

"I have the feeling that there's an unpleasant chauvinistic stereotype lurking in your version of Twyla Belton's psychology. This beauty-and-the-beast business smacks a little too familiarly of the old rape fantasy that all of us penis-envying girls are supposed to take to bed with us each night."

"The beauty-and-the-beast business wasn't my idea," I said. "It was Twyla's. If you'd seen her drawings, you'd understand."

"Yes, but how can you be sure?" she said. "You could be projecting again, Harry. You know your X-rays came back and I think we know what your problem is."

I got up from the desk and said, "My problem is you."

"You can't leave your problems behind you," she called out as I headed for the door. "Where are you going anyway? It's nearly five o'clock?"

"I'm tired of speculation," I called back to her. "I'm going to do a little field research. Pay a couple of quick, supper-time visits to the first two men on our list. I'll be back by seven-thirty. Then we can pick up the question of my fantasies where we left it."

"Oh, goodie," she said.

12

GERALD ARNOLD, he of the fine old English name and denim escutcheon, lived in a rambling frame apartment house on Ogden Avenue, about two miles west of the library. It had been quite a nice house at one time. Three-story, vaguely colonial. With maid's quarters and a second kitchen and an upstairs ballroom with French doors looking out on the street. But like just about everything else in this country, it had fallen on hard times. The veranda needed a coat of paint. The guttering looked like a sleeve full of cigarette holes. And if that weren't enough to discourage any self-respecting apartment hunter, what I could see through the two bay windows would have made his heart sink. Woodwork that looked as if paint had been poured over it out of a bucket. Cracked ceilings. Floral wallpapering that was peeling away in jagged strips, the way wrapping gets torn off a cardboard box. Even the elm tree in the front yard was sick. Someone had cut back the leafless branches like they were pruning a shrub and marked the trunk with a yellow X for the tree surgeons. It was a burnt-out, discouraged-looking spot; and as I sat looking at it from the front seat of the Pinto, I thought through what I was going to say to the burnt-out case who was living there.

It wouldn't do to tell Gerald Arnold that I was a private investigator. Not until I was certain he wasn't the guy I was after. I certainly didn't want to scare the Ripper into thinking he was being watched. There was no telling what that might do to a mind like his. I just wanted to identify him and to have him sit tight long enough for Al Foster and his forensic team to make an air-tight case for the grand jury. So what I needed was a legitimate excuse to come calling at dinner time. Something that would get me through the door and give me a few minutes to look Gerald Arnold and his rooms over.

I took another look at the house and asked myself what alias would appeal to a hippie living in a run-down apartment. And it came to me effortlessly. Housing inspector. Housing inspector investigating a complaint against the landlord filed by one of the other tenants. If I knew his type, it would be perfect. And it would also give me a reason to explore his rooms. I debated about whether I should pull the Colt Commander from the gun rack beneath the dash board. It was probably the prudent thing to do. But then I didn't expect to be put in a position where I might have to use it. Not if I played my cards right. And having it around might just tempt me into overplaying the hand. So

I left it where it was, cracked open the door and walked up the cement path to the stoop.

I got the name of one of the tenants from the old iron mailboxes hung beside the hall door. Ms. Clio Rosen sounded feisty enough. And I found the name of the realty company, Clancy & Sons, on a white placard taped beneath the mailboxes. I walked through the door into a dark corridor that smelled of cooking grease and mildew, then up six half-flights of rickety stairs, to the third-floor landing. According to the mailboxes, Gerald Arnold was 3-N. But I wouldn't have needed directions to find his rooms. Not when the northside door had a huge peace emblem spray-painted on its panels and a feathery white cross painted beneath it. I put on my most officious face, loosened my shirt collar, ruffed my hair a bit to suggest that I was coming to the end of a hard day, and knocked.

"Yeah, man?" a voice called from behind the door. It was a husky, soporific voice, as sluggish as a tortoise. I figured that Gerald Arnold was thoroughly stoned.

"Mr. Arnold?" I chirped. "Mr. Gerald Arnold?"

"Yeah?" he said in a sleepy drawl.

"My name is Stoner, Mr. Arnold. I'm with the metropolitan housing authority. We've had a complaint about the owner of this house. Clancy & Sons?" I took out my official detective's notebook and riffled a few pages to make it seem as if I was checking details. "A Ms. Clio Ross filed a complaint of neglect of property. I'm here to collect evidence for a condemnation hearing. I'd appreciate a few minutes of your time."

"They're going to condemn this place?" he said.

"That's what I'm here to determine."

"Well, all right!" Gerald Arnold said. He flung the door open. "Come on in. I've got nothing to hide."

Gerald Arnold had the shaggy blonde mane and long, doleful face of a grocery-calendar Jesus. Dark, soulful eyes. Hollow cheeks. A thin mouth. And a scribble of yellow hair on his chin and above his upper lip. He was dressed in jeans and a checked, long-sleeved shirt rolled at the cuff; and he was wearing a heavy gold cross around his neck that caught the light from the naked bulb in the hallway. The room behind him smelled strongly of marijuana smoke. I could see a couple of roaches, lying like the burnt tatters of a love letter on a big black porcelain ashtray on the floor. It wasn't much of a room. Say twelve by twelve with a mantlepiece on the far wall, a painted-over gas outlet in the center of the ceiling, and a pair of big, old-fashioned radiators, twisted like inductor coils, beneath the window to the left of the door. Three kitchen plates were set beneath the radiators to catch the overflow when the pipes were bled; a small calico cat was lapping furiously from another plate, propped on a painted table next to the radiators. The rest of the furniture in the room, what there was of it, was Heart Mart stuff. Two stuffed chairs with sprung cushions. A mattress with a Madras throw lying in front of the windows. An end table at the foot of the mattress, stacked with six or seven books. The one on top had a cross embossed on the cover. There were three pictures of Christ set like family portraits on the mantlepiece.

Arnold caught me staring at the pictures and said, "Heavy, huh?"

"Heavy," I said.

"You into Christ?" he said earnestly and bounced up and down on his toes. "I am. I'm born again, man. Honest! He changed my life."

Gerald pulled a sheaf of pamphlets from a drawer in the painted table and handed them to me.

"Read them. They'll do you good, man. I got plenty more, so you can keep them. God loves us all, brother. Even that son-of-a-bitch landlord of mine."

I could see that He hadn't completely changed Gerald's life. And on closer inspection, one of the portraits of Jesus turned out to be a photograph of Eric Clapton. Which was O.K. by me. Because I kind of liked Gerald Arnold, with his pamphlets and his profanities and his funny way of bouncing on the balls of his feet, as if he were getting set to go into the Big Game on God's Side.

I pretended to inspect the apartment, while Gerald bent my ear about Jesus and about what a wreck his life had been before he found Him.

"I'm from Detroit, man. Some heavy dudes in Detroit. Real hard-ass town. Had to get out of there, man. Had to!"

He started bouncing up and down so quickly that I began to suspect that born-again Gerry wasn't above taking a taste of meth from time to time. Say every four hours. He was haggard-looking enough to be a speed freak. And his teeth were discolored, which could have been from meth. Or just poor health habits, Harry, like it used to say on your grade-school report card. Either way, I didn't have to pump him for information. He just kept right on talking about himself, answering every question I could have put to him without making me open my mouth. It appeared Gerald had been in a motorcycle gang, the Silver Horsemen, up in Motor City. Riding the midwest with a chain belt and a denim vest full of uppers. And just generally having a good ol' time, terrorizing small town cops and stomping on rival gangsters. Until one fine day, two years before, his best friend, Mickey had stomped on him. What a falling off was there!

"Man, he almost blew me away," Gerald said. "I mean for all time. And I *loved* that dude. Like a brother, man. I

106

mean it was heavy. Took me almost a year to get my shit together after that. Wandered around some. Like I was in a daze, you know? Finally came down here to work at the Ford plant with another buddy. Only the foreman on the night shift starts riding me about my hair. Can you believe that shit, man? It got so bad I had to wear a hair net. Like a fucking girl. I mean I was ready to kill somebody — I was so messed up. And then I met Brother Thomas Stearns at a union meeting about nine months ago. Man, he just turned my life around. Got me into reading books, man. And going to church. And now, man, when that asshole foreman starts riding me, you know what I do?" He grinned at me. "I just flash him the other cheek, man! Wow, that burns him up!"

I laughed. I couldn't help it.

"You want to hear how I got turned on to Christ?"

I shook my head. I didn't think I could take a blow-by-blow account of Gerald's rebirth. Anyway, after listening to him talk for more than ten minutes, I was fairly well satisfied that he wasn't my man. For one thing he wasn't quiet enough. For another, speed freak or not, he was too damn normal at heart. And for a third, when I asked him if he ever thought of getting back at his friend, Mickey, for beating him up, he snorted and said, "Are you shitting me? This guy would make you look like a fire plug."

That didn't sound like a man who thought he was invincible. In fact, most of what Gerald Arnold said made him sound eminently vincible. Just a cheerful hop-head who thought he'd found his niche with the Almighty. Which was all right, too. So I looked him in the eye and said, "Do me a favor, Gerald?"

He said, "Sure!"

"Roll up your sleeves."

"My sleeves?"

He shrugged and rolled up his sleeves. Both forearms were as unmarked as a baby's bottom.

"Are you a cop?" he said. "I mean if you're a cop, I'm clean, man. You can see for yourself. No tracks. I don't even pack works anymore. Not since I was saved. I mean I know it must sound corny, but I kicked, man. Cold-turkey. I still get high on grass. But no more hard stuff. Honest!"

I wasn't sure whether I believed that or not. I'd never talked to an addict who hadn't just kicked or wasn't about to. But Gerald seemed to believe it. And if it made him feel good to think that God had helped him straighten up, I wasn't going to argue with him.

"That's really something," I told him.

Gerald Arnold wiped a loose strand of blonde hair from his wan, apostle's face, nodded solemnly, and said, "Praise God, it is."

13

I LEFT Gerald to his new life and walked back down the stairwell to the street. If they're all as easy as that, Harry, I said to myself, you could wrap this thing up by tomorrow night.

The sun was setting behind the rooftops and oak trees on the west side of Ogden, and the air had a vivid, velvety feel to it, the way it feels after a hard spring rain. I glanced at my watch. It was a quarter to seven. I spent a moment sitting on the car seat, taking in the night air. A black kid in a striped T-shirt and jeans sauntered by, a transistor radio to his ear. He had a big afro comb in one of his back pockets and a can of beer in the other. He pulled the beer can out, still shuffling to the tinny beat of the radio, took a quick sip, and wedged the can back in his pocket. I grinned at him, but he didn't see me.

Ah, Harry, I thought. And sighed peacefully. It was one of those moments, and God knows they're rare enough in my life, when I felt perfectly content. I liked the smell of the evening and the funny cool of the black kid with the radio and the beer can and the nervous patter of Gerald Arnold, the bemused Jesus-freak. It seemed worse than a shame to spoil it all by going back to work. But Haskell Lord only lived three blocks east of Ogden on Stettinius. And it was on my way back to the library. And if I was as lucky with Mr. Lord as I'd been with Gerald Arnold, I could go back to Kate Davis with the good news that two of our suspects had been eliminated. But, oh, the feel of the night wind and the look of the oak trees in the sunset.

I turned on the ignition and pointed the Pinto east, toward Stettinius.

It was nearly dark when I pulled up in front of the Lord home. But there was still enough blue light left in the sky to see that this was a very different neighborhood than Ogden Street. Lawns so trim they looked barbered. Newspapers piled neatly beside wire trash bins. The smell of burning leaves in the air like a peppery cologne and somewhere, in a back-yard arbor, the anise-scent of sweet goldenrod. The night air was so rich-smelling it cheered me up again. And then the look of the Lord home itself was modestly reassuring.

No peeling paint here. No ragged guttering. Just a two-story red brick house with a pitch roof and white Williamsburg trim, as solid and decent-looking as a cedar chest. Planters in the windows. A stone stoop with glass inserts on either side of the front door and a pearly white facade

110

above the doorway, shaped like a fluted scallop shell. There were no lights on in the front windows and the top floor was curtained, but I could see a yellow, prismatic glow through the inserts on either side of the door. Maybe from the dining room, where Haskell and the rest of the family were gathered about the table.

According to my notes, Haskell Lord was a little older than my other suspects. Twenty-seven. And while there was no occupation listed on Miss Moselle's card, he was either living with his parents or doing pretty well for himself, because that house and the yard that stretched out behind it was prime property. Jessie had remembered him as being a ruddy, quick-tempered fellow. The type who might not take kindly to a dinner-time visit. On the other hand, it was my best chance of catching him at home. Telephone solicitors know that. So do process-servers and private detectives. I ran through my repetoire of aliases once again. Decided that housing inspector wouldn't do. And any kind of salesman, magazine to insulation, would get the boot. Then I remembered what Jessie Moselle had said about the notice she'd been forced to send him and thought, why not? I could simply tell him the truth. That I was employed by the library and was investigating the disappearance of several books he had taken out. There had been some mix-up in the library records and I was just checking to see if he had returned them on time. And if he asked, why me? I could always bring up the final notice that had been sent to him several months before. It would give me an excuse to take a quick look at him and, if I were really lucky, to spot the tattoo on his forearm. I didn't feel the need to examine the interior of the house, although certain kinds of solid Republican decency can be a lot more disturbing than the run-down pad of a born-again hippie.

I took out my trusty notebook, smoothed my hair, rebut-

111

toned my shirt and stepped up the stone walkway to the front door. The doorbell went off as if it were set in a steeple. Bing-bang-bong! A minute or so passed and, just as I was about to ring again, the door opened.

I looked at the arms before I looked up at the face, only this guy was wearing a white Angora sweater. And his face was fair, freckled, and affable-looking. I did a bit of a double-take and wondered if I'd gotten the wrong address.

"Does Haskell Lord live here?" I asked the kid, who was about twenty-three and as decent-looking as the house he was living in.

"He used to," he said with a slight hesitation in his voice, as if Haskell's whereabouts was not something he cared to talk about. Then he smiled to show that he'd meant no hard feelings. "I'm his brother Jake. Who are you?"

"My name is Stoner. I work for the Hyde Park Library."

"Oh, yeah?" Jake said. "Up on Erie, huh?"

"That's the one. I was hoping I could talk to your brother about some books he took out. Do you have any idea when he might be back?"

"Well, to tell you the truth . . . " Jake said. And before he could finish, a very proper, silver-haired woman in a high-collared print dress appeared at the door. She was wearing square, tinted glasses with her initials, R.L., spelled out in tiny zircons at the bottom of each lens. Behind them, her eyes glittered like hard blue stones in a jewelry store window. Something about those eyes and the stiff-necked way she was holding herself told me she was expecting trouble. What kind I didn't know.

"What is it, Jacob?" she said in a clipped, nervous voice. "What's going on?"

Jacob gave me a cute conspiratorial wink and said, "Mom, this is Mr. Stoner. He works for the library."

Mrs. Lord seemed to relax a bit. "Well, why don't you tell Mr. Stoner we're eating?"

"He's looking for Haskell, Mom," Jacob said in a long-suffering voice.

Mother Lord's face trembled momentarily. It was the exact look that hard-nosed men get on their faces when they're trying to bite back grief. It was a damn interesting look and it made me curious. I decided, on the spot, to change my tack.

"It's really rather important that I speak to your son, Mrs. Lord. He could be in some trouble."

That was it. That was the word she'd been waiting to hear. That was the worry I'd seen in her face when she'd come to the door.

"What sort of trouble?" she said in a broken voice and reached for Jacob's hand.

He blushed a little and ducked his head, as if this were a scene he'd been through before.

"Mom," he said gently, "don't jump to conclusions. I mean this guy's from the library, not the police department. Just what is it you want?" He said it with authority, as if he were taking the part of his mother and his apparently trouble-prone brother.

"Maybe if I could come in?" I said.

Jake looked at his mother and she gave him a small nod.

"All right," he said. "We'll go to the den."

Jacob ushered me through a foyer flanked by a mahogany staircase, down a corridor, and into a den that looked rather like a fifties furniture showroom: blonde wood furnishings with chocolate-colored handles that looked like the buttons on a child's overcoat; a nubby orange couch that was merely an L-shaped frame meant for two sets of cushions; a striped armchair; a coffee table with seashells in a glass top; a pole lamp with two frosted glass shades; and a multicolored cotton rug, shaped like a place mat, in the center of the floor. Sitting in that room was like sitting in an Edsel, an experience vaguely embarrassing and borderline funny, except that there was nothing funny about the look on Mrs. Lord's face or about the photographs and trophies that crowded the walls and the mantle.

I thought at first they might have been Haskell's trophies or Jacob's. Then I saw the open plush velvet box on the mantle and the medal cushioned inside it, as if it were something to be picked up and admired. It was a purple heart with oak-leaf cluster. And the man in the pictures, the man who'd won the medal and the trophies and who smiled down handsomely from every wall as he must have smiled in life, was Captain Herbert Lord, U.S.N.

Mrs. Lord caught me looking at one of the trophies and sighed.

"My husband was a very courageous man," she said. "Sometimes I wish he was still here to help me, to lend me some of his strength. He died when Haskell was only ten years old. Jacob was only six. It's been very difficult to raise two boys on my own. I know I've made mistakes, but . . ." Her face trembled again and brother Jake made soothing noises.

"Just what's Hack supposed to have done?" he said belligerently.

"I'm not sure he's done anything," I said and started to feel a little guilty about the crisis I'd caused, even though I had the feeling that the mother was attuned to crisis, that she'd given her "lend me your strength, Herbert" speech like grace at every meal. Still, it made me uncomfortable to see her choking back tears. It made me uncomfortable to sit in that fifties room with all those pictures of Captain

114

Lord on the walls. So uncomfortable that I decided to level with them. "There's been some trouble at the library. Some trouble about books that Haskell took out. I just want to ask him a few questions."

Then something very odd happened. Instead of looking relieved as I thought she would, the mother began to sob.

"Oh, Jesus," Jake said under his breath. "For crying out loud, Mother, he hasn't done anything!" He turned to me with embarrassment and tried to explain. "You've got to excuse her, Mr. Stoner. She just doesn't understand the impression she makes. Haskell's . . . well, he's gotten into trouble in the past." Jake glanced at his mother and said, "Not all of it was his doing." He looked back at me. "Mom just assumes the worst every time somebody comes looking for him."

"Where is he, Jake?"

He blushed and said, "I'm not sure. We haven't seen him in awhile."

"How long a while?"

"Over two years. He moved out two years ago. To tell you the truth," he said under his breath, "I didn't blame him."

"Oh, you didn't!" Mrs. Lord said suddenly. "Well, I blamed him. I blamed him! My Jacob doesn't think his brother Haskell can make mistakes. He thinks everything Haskell has done is right and everything I've done is wrong."

"You know I didn't say that. I just meant I could understand why he might want to move out."

"And not talk to his mother or the brother who loves him?"

It was degenerating into a low-grade family argument, one that I didn't particularly want to witness. I started to

115

get up and the woman said, "Wait! Don't leave, Mr. Stoner. Don't leave until you've heard why my son Haskell decided to move away from our home."

"Mother," Jake said. "I'm not going to listen to this."

"Then, don't!" she said imperiously. "Haskell left us because of a girl." She laughed with a funny bitterness. "Did I say girl? She's a forty-five-year-old woman. A tramp, pure and simple. Low-life. She's the reason Haskell chose to leave us. She's the reason he never calls. What do you think of that, Mr. Stoner? A twenty-seven-year-old boy running around with a white-trash woman who's old enough to be his mother?"

I didn't say anything.

Mrs. Lord got up from the couch and walked over to the mantlepiece. She plucked a photograph in a small oval frame from the little garden of photographs growing there like Boston ferns. "It's a good thing that his father can't see him now," she said, staring at the picture. Her lip trembled, whether in anger or pity I couldn't tell. I imagined that would always be a hard thing to tell about Mother Lord, whose feelings seemed to run in a narrow circuit that led constantly back to her—what the world had done to her. "I have two sons," she said. "One of them has given me nothing but joy. He's made me proud of him. The other." She shook her head despairingly. "Haskell has been in and out of trouble since he was fourteen years old. And I'm tired of lying for him and making up excuses. If there's been some trouble at your library, Mr. Stoner, it wouldn't surprise me in the least if Haskell were the cause. He doesn't have that terrible mark on his arm for no reason."

I felt a chill run up my spine. "What mark?" I said and tried to sound casual. But she heard through it to the real excitement underneath.

"A mark," she said vaguely. "A tattoo he got in the Navy."

116

"Could I see the photograph, Mrs. Lord?"

She looked over at Jacob, who'd sunk into a kind of indignant silence since his mother had begun her embarrassing monologue. "I guess you can," she said, trying to build up her nerve. "Certainly you can. If he's done something wrong, he should be punished for it."

She thrust the photograph at me, as if she were renouncing responsibility for the boy it pictured. And I took a long look at him. He was standing beside his brother Jacob in what was probably a gym or a weight room. They were both the same height and they were both stripped to the waist. But that's where the resemblance ended. It was like a before-and-after picture for a muscle-building program. Jacob, blonde and skinny, with a tiny grin on his boyish face that indicated he was all too aware of the puny contrast he made to his muscle-bound brother, who was built like a miniature Hercules—huge biceps, huge pectorals narrowing to a wasp waist. Haskell was smiling, too, with amused tolerance at his kid brother. But it wasn't his build or his sleepy-eyed smile that chilled me. It was the tattoo on his right forearm, only half-visible in the photograph because he was resting that arm on Jacob's shoulder. I couldn't see all of the design. Just the serpent's fanged head coiled about the head of a woman and the first two letters of the slogan printed beneath it. E . . . V . . .

I took another look at his face. To fix it in my mind. The eyes, heavy-lidded as a reptile's and as coal-black as the hair. And the tight little mouth that smiled without pleasure —a bully's quick, triumphant grin. Then I handed the photograph back to the mother.

"It's extremely important that I locate your son, Mrs. Lord," I said.

She'd been watching me as I examined the photo and I could tell from the look on her face that, in spite of what

117

she'd said, she wasn't ready to cut the family ties. She clasped the picture to her breast as if she were reclaiming Haskell as one of her own and said, "What has my boy done?"

She wouldn't have been unhappy to have heard that he'd stolen something or committed some minor mischief. But she wasn't ready to hear the truth. Neither was Jacob, who'd perked up in his chair. He stared at me with a kind of forlorn hope, as if he were praying that I'd tell his mother once and for all that Haskell wasn't the black demon she'd made him out to be. But I couldn't tell her that. So I told her some books had been stolen, and she turned to Jacob with a look of vindication on her face that had to have been seen to have been believed. My heart went out to the kid, who slumped back haplessly in his chair.

"If he should get in touch with you, Mrs. Lord, I'd appreciate a call."

"Of course," she said smartly.

"And this woman you mentioned before. You wouldn't know her name, would you?"

"I certainly would," she said. "Effie. Effie Reaves. I don't know where she lives—these people move around so much. But she's somewhere in the county. At least her family is. She has a brother who owns a service station in Dent. Norris Reaves. You might try out there."

I thanked her and walked to the door.

14

I WAS half-way down the walk when Jake came running up behind me.

"Mr. Stoner?" he said. "Wait a second."

I stopped and waited for him to catch up with me. I could tell from the agonized look on his face that he was going to apologize—for his mother and for his brother, Hack. He was a polite, good-hearted kid, Jacob was, and I felt bad for him that he'd had the luck to have been born into that ill-starred family.

"Hack's in real trouble, isn't he?" he said with half a heart. "I mean, more than just stolen books?"

I said, "Yeah, Jake. He could be in real trouble."

"It's *her* fault," he said between his teeth. "Nothing he ever did was right. Nothing was ever good enough. And he tried, Mr. Stoner. He really tried to please her. Then I guess he just couldn't try anymore." He looked down at the walk and I looked down, too. "I guess I'd better level with you," he said after a moment. "That woman, Effie, she's kind of a tough case like Mom said. Into drugs and stuff like that. I could never figure out what Hack saw in her. Their relationship wasn't a bit romantic. I don't think Hack ever felt that way about a girl. Not after what he went through with *her.*" He glanced back at the doorway. "I'm just trying to tell you that if Hack did something wrong, it wasn't all his fault. He just didn't have much of a chance. Especially after getting drummed out of the service and tying up with that Reaves woman and her crowd. After he met her, he went all to hell. So I hope you'll take that into consideration if you do catch up with him."

I said, "Thanks, Jake. I'll do that."

"One thing, though," he said as he turned to go back to the house. "Hack's got a real short temper. He's had it since he was a kid. He just never seems to know his own strength. I guess that's one reason he's always getting into trouble. You're a pretty big man—a lot bigger than he is. But Hack's been pumping iron since he was twelve and he's stronger than anybody I know. Effie's a pretty rough lady, too. So if I were you, I'd be careful."

I told him I would.

The library lot was virtually deserted when I pulled up to the rear doors at a quarter past eight. I got out of the car and listened to the night sounds. Loose leaves were skittering across the tarmac, making a dismal, grating noise like the sound of a rake being dragged across concrete. Or maybe the rattle of a skeleton in a closet? Because that's what I'd been thinking about. Skeletons and Haskell Lord, with his heavy-lidded snake's eyes and his tight bully's mouth. And his forlorn brother, who'd wanted me to understand that it wasn't all Hack's fault—that even psychopaths, sex killers who crumple up little girls like paper bags, have family problems. And hard-bitten mothers in print housedresses who are willing to believe the worst about their sons but are unwilling to accept responsibility for helping to make them into what they are. Or just the sweet part. The part that makes them feel like they've done their all and been miserably repaid for their effort. There was probably real tragedy in there somewhere, in among the skeletons in the Lord family closet. Only I couldn't seem to find it. Because every time I started thinking about Hack Lord, I'd remember Twyla and the library books and what he was planning to do. And it would make me shiver as I had in that strange den, when I'd seen the picture of the snake gliding across his arm as if it were readying itself to strike again.

I walked through the chattering leaves and into the library, where Kate Davis and Miss Moselle stood gossiping in front of the circulation desk. The place looked eerie that late at night, with the big white lights pooling dully on the empty tabletops and collecting on the carpeting the way sunlight collects on a road bed. But then any place but my own apartment would have looked a little eerie after what I'd seen in the Lord home. And suddenly I wanted to get back to my two-and-a-half rooms. To get back there with Kate Davis and to make a little, uncomplicated love. If there is such a thing. To show some tenderness to her and to be shown tenderness in return. That's exactly what I want, I said to myself. That and a drink or two to wash the ugliness of the Lord house as far out of my life and out of Kate's life as I could.

"You look positively beat," she said to me as I walked up to her. "Did something go wrong?"

"You could say that. I think I found the Ripper."

Her blue eyes got very large behind the tortoiseshell glasses and her little mouth fell open noiselessly. "You found him?" she said breathlessly.

"His name is Haskell Lord. Hack, for short. I saw a photograph of him and he has the snake tattoo. He also has just about every other problem that Benson Howell said he would have. Broken home. Nasty, overweening mother. A history of violent behavior. Some pretty crummy friends. You name it. About the only thing that Hack Lord had going for him since he was ten years old was his brother's love. And that apparently wasn't enough."

"My God," Kate said. "Did you see him? Was he in the house?"

"No. They aren't sure where he is. That's what I've got to look into tomorrow."

"Some prospect," she said grimly. "I think you need a drink."

"Many drinks. And would you mind if we went to my place? I don't think I could take a lot of strangers tonight."

"Just one, maybe?" she said with a sweet, encouraging smile.

We got back to the Delores at nine. I called Al Foster and gave him Hack's name and description. He said he'd put out an A.P.B. That made me feel a little better. After a Scotch or two I felt better still. I stopped brooding about what to do with Haskell Lord and started enjoying Kate Davis, who was demonstrating surprising civilian skills for the great-grandaughter of an impetuous general. She made me scrambled eggs, à la M.F.K. Fisher, cooked in a cold skillet with a half-pound of butter for what seemed like an hour and a half. And it was good.

"Where'd you learn to cook?" I said to her.

She grinned at me and said, "I can even dress myself since they've given me back my belt and shoe laces."

Then she fixed me a hot toddy, à la *The New York Times Cookbook*. Rum and more butter and a cinnamon stick stuck in a cut-glass goblet. And it was good.

"Where'd you learn to mix drinks?" I said to her.

She grinned again. "Oh, I know lots of things. How to get tomato juice stain out of a wool sweater. How to darn a Gold Toe sock," she said, pulling at my foot.

"How 'bout making love?"

She nodded. "That, too."

"You'd make somebody a nice wife."

"Uh-uh." She shook her head and some of the playfulness went out of her smile. "I tried that route, Harry. For three years. And it's taken another three years to wash out the stain. You wonder where I got all those T.A. terms from? Well, buddy, it wasn't out of a book. I've been seeing a shrink since I left Ed. We're down to one meeting a month and I want to keep it that way. So no marriage. Not for this girl."

"You consult your shrink about *everything?*" I said.

"Not *everything,*" she said, mocking my tone of voice.

"How about me? You think I might come up?"

She laughed. "I'd be willing to bet on it."

She sat down on the couch and looked me over with a bright, lecherous eye. "Well, you've had your supper. And you had your hot toddy. What's left to do?"

I shrugged. "We could share intimacies again."

She shook her blonde head solemnly. "No. We've had enough of that, I think. At least for one day. You certainly have, haven't you?"

I thought of Haskell Lord and said, "Yeah."

"Anyway I've never been too high on sharing secrets. It reminds me of grade school when we all exchanged valentines. You know it was never the ones you got that caught at your heart. It was the ones you didn't get. The ones who forgot you or who you forgot. The past is too damn sad and small to share. So let's have what my shrink might call a 'now' experience. How does that sound?"

"O.K.," I said. "I like games. How does it work?"

"Close your eyes."

"I'm not sure I like those kind of games."

Kate winked at me and said, "You'll like this one."

I closed my eyes.

I don't know how she did it. I mean, of course, without making a sound. Whether she'd had that much practice or whether she was just being especially careful for me. But when she told me I could open my eyes again, she was sitting across the room on the baize armchair and her frilly white blouse and denim jeans, her bikini panties and her lacy brassiere were piled in a neat little stack on the bare wood floor.

She had a beautiful body and she was the sort of girl who knew it. Who didn't have to exaggerate by posturing or to play modest by hiding herself with a timid hand. No thrown-out chest, no sucked-in tummy for Kate Davis. She sat across from me as coolly as if she were fully clothed. And when she saw the look in my eye, she threw her head back and laughed.

"I told you you'd like this game," she said.

124

"What happens next?"

"That, my dear," Kate Davis said, "is up to you."

"Then close *your* eyes."

She did as she was told. I walked over to the armchair and lifted her up. Her rear end was bumpy from the twill of the cushion. She wrapped her arms around my neck and whispered. "You really are old-fashioned, aren't you?"

"Not about everything," I said and carried her to the bed.

She made love expertly—fierce, competitive love that was exhilarating. Lovemaking that left us both exhausted. I hadn't felt that kind of excitement since I was a kid breaking into my first brassiere. And the lady seemed fairly well satisfied, too. Satisfied but, I thought, a little perplexed. A little remote. As if lovemaking weren't quite as uncomplicatedly joyous for her as it had been for me.

I stroked her blonde curls back from her forehead and pulled her beside me and *didn't* ask what it was, what sad song was playing in her head. Not that I didn't want to know. I did. But it was her grief and I learned a long time ago that when people want to be rescued they'll let you know. That when you butt in on your own, you're looking to soothe some pain inside of you—some sense of exclusion. I wanted her to "share intimacies," as she put it. But in her own time. Because this girl was special. She had her own quirky rhythms, her own hurky-jerky style of play. Sometimes funny and hurried-up. And at that moment, as she lay curled in my arms, very slow and serious.

So I held her and held my tongue. And after a time she turned in my arms so I could feel her breasts against my chest, hard-tipped and as round and firm as oranges. She reached up and brushed some of the sandy hair out of my face and wiped at my eyes as if she were brushing back tears.

"Goddamn it," she said softly. "I think Jessie was right. I think I *am* falling in love with you."

"Maybe you'll get over it," I said.

She made a sour face and said, "I don't think so. I know the symptoms too well."

"Well, if you're asking my opinion, I think it's a fairly good idea."

She shook her head. "It's a rotten idea."

"And why is that?"

"Because one of us will end up getting hurt."

There was no sense in pretending it wasn't possible. Maybe even probable, given the fact that both of us liked to have things our own ways. But, good Lord, love's as common as colds and we're just about as defenseless against it. Unless we turn into hermits or turn the impulse inward, twist it like a bramble, the way Haskell Lord had done, or treat it like a game, make it into a pleasure trip and when it stops being fun, when it starts becoming as compli- cated as the rest of life or when it starts making the rest of life look simple, call it quits. Some people can do that. Judging from the number of divorce cases I handle, a good number of people. But I can't. Or won't. Someone once told me that the two are one.

So I told her getting hurt was the chance we'd both have to take, which didn't seem to please her.

"Maybe you've never had a really painful relationship?" she said defensively. "Maybe that's why you can be so high- minded about it?"

I thought of Jo Riley and said, "You know what your

trouble is, Kate? You think you're the first lady since Eve who made a bad bargain and got burned for it."

She drew back in the bed. "You think I'm acting like a child?"

"No," I said. "I think you're treating me like one. I told you before. I can take care of myself. I *like* to take care of myself. In love or not."

She looked a little hurt and said, "You mean you're *not* in love with me?"

"Jesus," I said. "Let's drop the subject."

She laughed mildly and hooked her legs around mine.

"You're feeling better now?" I said.

She nodded. "Let's make love again, Harry," she said pulling me to her. "And talk about what it all means in the morning."

15

ONLY WHEN the morning came, there didn't seem to be any talk left in either of us. Maybe it was the look of the dreary sky. Or maybe it was just too early in the day for the "making commitments" scene she had planned. But as we sat on the couch, sipping hot coffee and reading the newspaper and generally acting like an old married couple at the start of a day, there was no talk larger than "Pass me the editorial page, would you?" or "I'll make you some coffee with egg shell in it one of these mornings," as if it had all been settled, miraculously, during the night—that we would live together and see how things went.

I would have preferred to talk it out. But I didn't force

the issue. Not simply for the sensible reason, for the adult reason that you can't make up another person's mind. But for the very selfish reason that I didn't want to scare Kate Davis away. I'd enjoyed making love to her more than I'd enjoyed anything in a long time. I liked the way she looked, blonde and pink in my terry robe as she sat beside me, reading the newspaper with her habitual look of high seriousness. I liked the seriousness itself, the willingness to mix it up in bed and out, and the sense of humor that accompanied it. I liked the lady enough not to risk loosing her to her past or to her hard-won sense of independence. So I pretended it had all been settled, too, and went about my early morning business.

I called Al Foster again and found out that Haskell Lord hadn't turned up. But Al had gotten the C.I.D. report and, for what it was worth, the only felons with that kind of tattoo on their arms were serving life terms in Lima. Which was just as well. I told him about Effie Reaves and her brother Norris. And he said to get back in touch if I got a lead. Then I pulled out the phone book and looked up Norris Reaves's auto repair shop. It was on Harrison Pike, about two miles outside the city limits on the western edge of town. Trying to find Hack Lord could be a long process, which was why Al was letting me do the spadework. And I figured that finding Reaves's sister would be a good first step. I jotted down the address of the garage, patted Kate on the cheek and said, "I'm going to get dressed."

She looked up at me bashfully. "About last night."

"What about last night?"

"It was really fine," she said. "That's all. As good as it's been since . . . well, since Ed and I fell out of love. Maybe it'll stay that way, for awhile at least."

I sat down beside her on the couch and had to fight the

impulse to cup her lovely face in my hands. It was the natural impulse, given the shy look of hopefulness on that face. But the gesture smacked too much of a chauvinism that I wanted to avoid. Besides, the truth was I didn't know anymore than she did whether we'd stay together for awhile or forever.

"I think it might," I said and realized I was picking my words the way a nervous man might pick through a plate of food. "We can try to make a go of it, Kate."

She smiled fecklessly and I thought, oh hell, Harry! and threw a lot of good adult reasoning out the window. "We'll make it last, Kate. I'll see to it."

"Promise?" she said with a small, unhappy laugh.

And I promised.

I dropped Kate off at the library and gave her a kiss goodbye. A sweet, passionate kiss.

"Wow!" she said.

"My words, too."

We weren't likely to see each other until well after nightfall. She had to canvas the six girls on Ringold's list, to find out if any of them had seen a black-haired, muscle-bound young man with a tattoo on his right forearm. And I had to run down Effie Reaves. So we kissed again, like a young married couple saying their first goodbye after the honeymoon, and wished each other luck. Then she headed into the library and I backed the Pinto onto Erie and drove west to Dana and the expressway.

It would be stretching a point to call Dent, Ohio, a town. You're in it before you realize it, straight off the Boulevard and up Race Road to the Pike; then you're past it a mile farther on, when Harrison dips down into the green, hilly countryside of north Hamilton County. A couple of two-pump gas stations, a tiny trailer park, a drive-in theater marked "Closed for the Season," a handful of go-go bars with signs that read "Girls, girls, girls!." All of this set on the shoulderless curbs of a mile-long stretch of highway is all there is to Dent, Ohio.

Norris Reaves Auto Repair Shop, which looked like a big, white slat barn, was located on the western fringe of the small commercial strip along Harrison Pike. It probably *had* been a barn at one time, because Dent marked the edge of farm country. The little township itself had been farm country not too many years before. Corn fields and blackberry patches and jagged stands of oak and maple that looked like puzzle pieces set out on a broad, dusty tabletop. The yard around the garage was littered with automobile parts, rusting axles, bald outsized truck tires, and old radiators lying like spent canteens on the hard dirt driveway that led up to the garage doors. I parked the Pinto behind a Harley-Davidson Electraglide that was propped beneath an oak tree, took a quick look at the sky, which was threatening rain, and walked up to the Reaves repair shop.

The big barn doors were open, but nobody seemed to be around. I stepped inside. There weren't any cars being serviced, but there were plenty of tools and parts lying about. Big workbenches full of them. Black hoses dangling on the walls like sausages. A portable hydraulic lift sitting in the center of the dirt floor. A big, gun-metal chest sitting beside it, with a couple of drawers pulled open and the tools inside shining like scalpels on a hospital tray. Chrome-plated reversible wrenches, lug nuts of every shape and size, screw drivers, wratchets, power drills. I

131

picked up one of the wrenches and looked it over. It still had the price sticker on its shank.

Whoever had bought those tools must have liked the way they sparkled. Either that or he had a lot of extra cash to spend. I dropped the wrench back in the chest and walked out into the yard and around the side of the building to the rear lot. Something was making a noise back there. A huffing sound that got louder as I rounded the corner. It wasn't until I was almost on top of him that I realized the sound wasn't coming from a piece of machinery but from a huge, red-haired man doing bench presses inside a little caged-off area behind the barn.

"Ouf-ouf-ouf." He grunted every time he lifted the bar. Which was Olympic size and loaded with three forty-five pound black iron disks on each end. That made two-hundred and seventy pounds, plus the bar, the man was pressing, which was enough to make Arnold Schwarzenegger groan. He was bare-chested and his abdomen looked like the carapace of a lobster—all rock-hard, etched, and segmented musculature.

"Jus' leave me finish this set," he called out to me. "Got three more reps to go."

He lifted the bar three more times and with each lift the muscles in his chest knotted up like wet, twisted towels and his biceps bulged as if there were grapefruits rolling beneath his flesh.

"Ouf!" the red-haired man grunted and lowered the bar into the prongs of the bench.

"Jus' working on my pecs," he said, poking one long finger into his chest. He moved up on the bench, his huge legs straddling either side, and continued to prod at the red swollen muscles, as if he'd lost feeling there and was trying to restore the circulation. He looked up at me and smiled cheerfully. His front two teeth were broken off at the gum; but, aside from that, his face had the gentle bovine look of a country boy. Long and dewy-eyed and easygoing.

"Just pumping up," he said as he worked on his pecs. "Going to do some dumbbell flyes next. Then bomb out on my lats. That is, if you don't have a problem that keeps me from it."

He got up from the bench and pulled a gray sweatshirt from where it was hung on the chicken wire cage. *Property Of O.S.U. Athletic Department,* it said on the front. The red-haired man did a check pose to impress me, laughed a little when I looked impressed, then slipped the shirt on.

"What kin I do for you?" he said as he walked from the cage.

Now I'm a pretty good-sized man. Six three, two-fifteen. No muscle-builder, but I stay in shape. Yet old Red, standing there in front of me, made me look the way Jake Lord had looked standing beside his brother, Haskell. I mean he dwarfed me. It couldn't have been a coincidence that he was a body-builder. Not after the picture I'd seen of Hack. So I figured this giant was Norris Reaves, Effie's brother. And judging from the quantity of equipment in the cage—bench press and barbells and flye-pulls and all of it relatively new—I figured that it was just possible that old Hack worked out there, too.

"Your car broke down?" he said. "I kin getchu a wrecker. But it's going to cost some."

"Looks like business is booming," I said, pointing at the equipment in the cage.

"I do all right," Norris said and frowned. "You got a car you want me to look at or what?"

133

"No car, Red. But I'd like to ask you a few questions."

"You kin ask," he said, flexing his right arm as if he were working out a cramp.

"I'm looking for a friend of yours."

"Yeah?" Reaves said. "Who might that be?"

"Haskell Lord."

He didn't say anything for a couple of seconds. Just chewed it over solemnly. Then he smiled as if to say it wasn't that big a deal. Only he'd thought it over a second too long for my liking. Besides he had a face like a mirror and anything as rare as a worrisome thought smoked it up like a dying man's breath. When a man that big and strong starts calculating, I wonder what he's toting up.

"Ain't seen Hack around here for awhile," Reaves said.

"How about your sister? Have you seen her?"

"Oh, sure. I see Effie all the time."

"I understand that she and Hack are friends."

"Could be," he said. "Where'd you hear all that?"

"From Hack's brother."

He mulled it over again. "You ain't a cop, are you?"

"Private investigator."

"Looking for Hack, huh?"

I nodded.

"Well, I can't tell you where he is, 'cause I don't know. But if you want to talk to Effie, I kin point her out to you."

"That would be a help," I told him.

"You know where Turkey Run Ridge is?" he said.

"I can find it."

He laughed, a big robust laugh of amusement at the city slicker. "You can, huh? Well, I don't doubt you, mister, but it's a might tricky getting there." He sighed and looked back at the cage, as if he wished he were inside doing

134

flye-pulls. "I guess I kin take a few minutes off to show you. Only I ain't got a car here. Just a cycle."

"My car's out front," I said. "You can ride with me or I can follow you."

He looked back one last time, over his enormous shoulder, at the cage where the dumbbells and weight disks were standing like cast-iron animals, and said, "All right, then. Just let me close up here. And I'll take you on over."

16

IF YOU'VE ever seen a grown man straddling a Shetland pony, you have some idea of what big Norris Reaves looked like hunched on the Harley. I followed that hulking figure as he burbled west down Harrison, past the I-275 interchange, and up into the autumn hills along the Whitewater River. About three miles out, he veered north onto an S-shaped, two-lane road that climbed through stands of maple and pine to a broad plateau dotted with farm houses. Farmland rolled and tumbled on either side of the roadbed, then the highway jogged east and started climbing again. I began to see Reaves's point about finding my way. The roads were like coils of rope tossed haphazardly on the hillsides. And I probably wouldn't have had a bit of trouble getting lost.

Two miles farther on, we came to an interchange. The main road continued eastward, while a gravel road ran north up the side of a hill. A street sign stuck in the dirt read *Turkey Run Ridge*. Reaves turned off on the side road. And up we went. The lane ran high above a huge forested valley, which lay beneath us on the west side of the road. A few ramshackle farmhouses were set on the east side, old frame houses and outbuildings weathered black by the wind. It was a rugged-looking spot for a lady to be living in. Rugged and remote as a Tennessee mountain road. But if what I'd heard about Effie Reaves were true, she was as tough as the landscape.

About a half mile farther on, Reaves pulled off the lane into a dirt yard in front of one of those ramshackle farmhouses. I slid in behind him. It was a one-story frame house with a roofed veranda in front and what looked like an old tobacco-colored barn set about a hundred yards behind it, at the foot of a gentle hill. A dirt path led down the hillside to the barn and another path led up to the front steps of the house. A porch swing dangling from the veranda roof was creaking in the wind.

As I got out of the car, Reaves walked up to the porch and bellowed, "Effie!"

A spatter of cold rain kicked at the dust in the front yard and peppered the Pinto's roof like a handful of shot. I pulled my coat lapels around my neck and waited by the car while Reaves searched the house. I heard him holler "Effie!" a couple more times, then he came back out the door and stood on the porch, with his big hands on his hips and a look of blank perplexity on his farmboy's face.

"Now where the hell's she got to?" he said in a voice that

was probably meant to be a thoughtful whisper but which boomed out across the desolate yard like a thunderclap. He walked down the steps and looked around the house, as if he thought she might be hiding, like a sleepy dog, behind the latticework under the porch. The cold rain was coming down pretty heavily. It had soaked Reaves's sweatshirt as soon as he stepped beyond the overhang, plastering it against his massive chest and torso. I had given up trying to keep dry and started to worry about keeping warm. The wind was so cold it made my teeth chatter and my breath hang in white clouds in the rainy air.

"Maybe she's gone down to the barn to look after the goats," Reaves said without much conviction. "We can take a look."

He walked across the yard, taking big, bear-like strides, and down the hard dirt pathway to the barn. I followed him down a hillside that was littered with stones and choked with weeds. A single sunflower fluttered in the wind like a pennant. The ground flattened out in front of the barn; I could hear the goats bleating noisily inside. Reaves pulled one of the big slat doors open and shouted, "My's well come in out of the rain."

I walked into the barn, which smelled of hay and goat turds and wood dust. There were a couple of horse stalls on my right, just empty bins half-filled with feed, a big hay loft overhead dripping with straw and rain water, and a goat shed on my left where two barrel-chested nanny goats were sitting out the storm. A shovel and a pitchfork were hung neatly on the unopened barn door behind me.

Reaves looked around the empty barn and shrugged. "Hell if I know where she's got to," he said crankily.

He walked across the packed dirt floor and looked out the open door at the rain. Then he reached to his right and pulled the shovel from its hook. He turned back to me and said, "What do you want to find Hack for, anyway?"

"I told you. I want to ask him some questions. The fact is he could be in some trouble with the law."

For the second time since I'd met him, Norris Reaves paused to think things out. And for the second time since I'd met him, I wondered why. Wondered and worried a bit, because I wasn't armed and he was as big as they come. You're getting pretty paranoid, Harry, I said to myself. But it didn't feel like paranoia. Men like Reaves shouldn't have to think about questions or answers. Not unless those questions or answers could get them into trouble.

He propped his arm on the shovel handle, like a bizarre version of *American Gothic,* and took a deep breath.

"Maybe he don't want to answer your questions," he said.

"Why don't we ask him and see?"

"Like I said. I don't know where he is."

"But your sister does."

Reaves took another deep breath and his chest heaved. "What you want to go making trouble for, mister?" he said almost sulkily. "What do you want to bring the law down on us for?"

I'd had enough of that barn and of Norris Reaves. I started toward the door.

"No," he said and held the shovel out to block my way. "I can't take the chance. That fucking speed freak could get the lot of us busted if he starts talking to the law."

I stared blankly at the shovel and felt the fear start up in the pit of my stomach. "You're kidding, aren't you?" I said to him.

He shook his head very slowly and motioned with the shovel head toward the rear of the barn. It was one of those nightmare moments when you know things are getting out of hand and you don't know why.

"I don't know what you think's going on here, Red," I said, and the smile I made felt pasty even to me. "But I'm investigating a girl's murder and all I want to do is ask Haskell a few questions." I pointed at the shovel. "There's no need for that. Why don't we just call this whole thing off before somebody gets hurt."

"Ain't nobody going to get hurt but you," he said placidly. He poked the shovel at me and I stepped back toward the goat shed. "I don't like people snooping around. That's one thing I don't like." He jabbed at me again with the shovel and I almost lost my footing as I backed away from him. "I'm going to fix you first, then I'm going to scare up that no-good son-of-a-bitch Hack and fix him, too. If I fix things right, there won't be nobody else coming around here and messing with my business."

He'd backed me up a good twenty feet from the door, and the look on his long, country boy's face was absolutely vicious, as if I'd said something against him or his family— pure, feuding mean. I didn't understand the look and I didn't understand the spot I was in, but that didn't make it any less frightening.

"Look," I said desperately. "I don't care about your business. I told you I'm only interested in Hack."

He shook his head stubbornly. "I can't be sure you'll kill him if you find him; and once you get that boy talking, there ain't going to be no stopping him. That's just the way it is with speed freaks. Wired the way they are, they got to move their mouths to keep from bugging out." He sighed almost piteously. "It ain't as if I didn't warn him not to take the stuff. But he's never been right in the head, that one. Not

140

him or his whole damn family. It just ain't good business to eat up your own profits."

"Speed?" I said hollowly. "You deal speed?"

"Me and Effie and Hack too, when he's sober. Took me a goddamn extension course at O.C.A.S. to figure out how to do the bookkeeping and administration. I got a growing concern, mister, and I ain't about to let nobody fuck it up."

I suppose his entrepreneur's pride would have been funny if he weren't holding that shovel in his huge hand. At least I'd begun to understand what I'd gotten myself into, and somewhere in the back of my mind I was thinking that, wired on speed, Hack Lord was going to be one dangerous man to track down. But at that moment, Hack Lord wasn't the problem. I thought about all those chrome-plated wrenches and almost laughed. I was about to be "fixed" so that Goodman Reaves could keep on buying dumbbells and power saws.

"I don't care if you deal speed," I said to him. "Can you understand that?"

"Oh, I understand, all right," he said. "You're probably telling the truth, too. But the law's not going to see it your way and I got a business to protect. If Hack's killed him a girl—and I sure as hell wouldn't put it past him—then the law's got to be in on this, sooner or later, no matter how you look at it. They find you and Hack dead—under the right circumstances—they might figure you and him killed each other, and then maybe they'll leave us alone. It ain't a sure thing, mind you. But I've been thinking it out, analyzing it, and there just ain't no other solution. You got to go and so does Hack. Nothing personal, mister. I guess it just ain't your day."

I swallowed hard and couldn't think of one thing to say.

It wouldn't do me any good to point out the flaws in his logic. He didn't have a complicated mind, just a deadly one, as lethal and efficient as a twenty-five cent rattrap. And me . . . well, I'd just happened in at the wrong moment. Like he said, it wasn't my day.

Reaves took the shovel in both hands, sank it into the dirt floor, and kicked the spade with his foot, sending a big chunk of dirt flying past me. I jumped back and he laughed to himself, as if making people jump were his idea of a good joke. He jerked the spade out of the ground and jabbed it back into the hole he was digging.

"What are you doing?" I asked with a shudder.

"What's it look like?" he said without looking up. "I'm digging a grave."

"Why?" I said.

He didn't answer. Just kept digging. Long, fluid jabs with the spade, as if he were working on his pecs again.

Ka-chunk. Ka-chunk.

For a second I couldn't think at all. For a second I was back in 'Nam, on recon, and my heart was pounding and the adrenalin was flowing and all of my brains were up in my eyes and in my ears. Then I got angry. Not with Reaves. Not a first. With myself, for leaving the .45 in the car under the dash when I'd known full well that something wasn't right about that garage and about the man who'd stopped to think as soon as I'd mentioned Haskell Lord. Then it all came down to the sound of that spade biting into the ground and the look on Norris Reaves's bland, country boy's face. I stopped riding myself and started hating him and the sound he was making. And within a second or two, I had enough anger going to turn that adrenalin to good use. I began to think again, with a stoned-out, crystal clarity. To plan how to get to that gun and to shoot that big bastard with it before he stuck me into that hole he was digging.

I looked quickly around the barn. Reaves was standing about ten feet in front of the open door, right in the center of the doorway. I was about ten feet behind him and another twenty feet from the rear wall. There were a couple of boarded-up windows on that wall. And the rear doors were barred and nailed shut. I couldn't go away from him or around him; so it had to be through him. And that meant moving him out of the doorway, to the right or to the left, then somehow turning him around long enough for me to get past him and get a headstart up the hill. There was just no way I could take him on head-on. His wrists were the size of my forearms.

He could see I was thinking it over and he smiled again, almost angelically, as if he thought the idea that I wanted to save my skin was kind of cute, like baby's first word. I backstepped to my left, toward the goat shed, and he followed me with his eyes, his hands still pumping with machine-like regularity at the hole in the barn floor.

"I wish you wouldn't do that," he said in a soft voice. "It makes me kind of edgy. And you wouldn't like me when I'm edgy. Believe me."

I wanted to make him edgy, all right. That huge, muscle-bound man who thought that killing another human being wasn't "personal." I wanted to make him so edgy that he'd charge me like a mad bull. Unthinkingly, depending solely on brute strength. He already had strength and position. All I had going for me was speed. And that was no sure thing. I wanted to even up the odds. I wanted to make Norris Reaves at least as mad as I was. Then I might be able to side-step him.

The spade went, "Ka-chunk!"

143

I looked him over and decided that ruffling him wouldn't be hard. It was just a question of finding his weakest point and then making the taunting as crude and vicious as I could. And with a muscleman, weak points are easy to find. They wear their vanity like armor all over their bodies. I took a deep breath and started up.

"You got a girl, Red?"

He kept digging.

"I've often wondered about that. Whether or not guys like you had girlfriends. I mean, all that work you do in the gyms. All those flye-pulls and bench presses. You've got to be trying to impress somebody. So why do you do it if you don't do it for the girls?"

He didn't look up.

"Or maybe you don't like the girls. Is that it, Red? Is that why you oil down your 'pecs' and your 'lats'? It's not for the girls is it, Red? It's for the boys. The young boys. So they'll start dragging around after you with their hands in their pants. Do you like that, Red? A big, ugly guy like you? When the fags come on to you?"

"Just keep talking, mister," he said and slammed the spade with his foot. "I like to hear you talk like that."

"I'll bet you do, Red. An ugly guy like you probably likes to hear about the boys. Do you hang out at the Y, Red? Do you go into the steam rooms and flex your muscles? Or do you go to the parks, Red? Do you go into the johns and pretend to take a pee and wait for the teenage kids to come in so you can show off for them? I guess you must have to wear a bag over that head of yours. But they're not really interested in your face, are they, Red?"

Reaves took a deep breath and the muscles in his huge chest jumped as if they'd been touched with a cattle prod. "You better shut up, now, mister," he said with an eerie softness. "If you know what's good for you."

"Why? You got a hot date waiting for you back at some bar? Is that it? Some guy you want to corn-hole, so it'll make you feel like a he-man?" I laughed an ugly laugh. "All the muscles in the world wouldn't make you a man, Red. You got faggot written all over you."

He stopped shoveling and I tensed to move.

Reaves pulled the spade out of the ground and juggled it in his right fist, as if it were a handful of change. "I warned you," he said. "But you jus' wouldn't listen."

His face had gotten very red, almost as red as his hair. And he was breathing hard, with the dumb fury of a cornered animal. He took the shovel in both hands and snapped the handle in two with a single movement of his arms. It cracked with the sound of a gunshot. Jesus! I said to myself and stepped back quickly to my right. He tossed the shovel head behind him and waved the broken length at me like a club.

"I'm going to make you beg me to stop hurting you," he said.

He dropped into a crouch and came at me, tossing the handle from hand to hand.

I crouched, too. And when he was about ten feet away, I jumped to my right, toward the door. He adjusted more quickly than I thought he would, given all those muscles. But you have to sacrifice something to develop a physique like his, and I knew from that one movement that I had better than a step in speed on him.

I feinted to my left, and he whipped that shovel handle out and slashed at my right shoulder. The broken end caught my sleeve and ripped it open. I moved back to my right and he crept forward, swinging the club across the front of his body. I backstepped again and knew that I was running out of room. The goat pen was right behind me.

Reaves stood up for a second and smiled, as if he thought

he had me trapped. There was about seven feet between us now; but I'd pulled him far enough away from the barn door so that, if I did manage to get around him, I could make it outside without any danger of him cutting me off.

"Well, c'mon, faggot," I said between my teeth.

He snarled furiously and came at me, the shovel handle raised above his head like a broad sword. I zagged left and he turned left; then I dove to my right, like I was following a sideline pattern, and made it past him just as he was bringing the shovel handle down into the fence around the goat pen.

The goats started bucking and shrieking. And so did Norris Reaves. "I'll kill you!" he screamed. "I'll kill you!"

He whirled around, but I was already three steps ahead of him, making straight for the barnyard. I thought I was out of immediate danger. I thought I had enough distance on him to make it up to the car. Then something struck me hard in the back and knocked me up against the closed side of the barn door. For a second I didn't know what had happened, didn't realize that he'd tossed that shovel handle at me like a brickbat and caught me right in the middle of the back. It was a costly second, because by the time I'd gotten my breath and turned to face him, he was only a few feet away and coming hard—his arms spread apart and his enormous shoulders tensed as if he were doing a crab pose.

I reached to my right and jerked the pitchfork off the wall and, without thinking about my aim, jabbed it forward just as Reaves got to me.

He shrieked with pain, but still managed to club me on the side of the head—hard enough to knock me down and almost out on the dirt floor. I lay there for a second, stunned. Don't pass out! I pleaded with myself. For God's sake, don't pass out! And I didn't, although it cost me

146

energy I didn't know I had to sit upright again. Reaves was lying on his back about five feet behind me, clutching at the pitchfork that was sunk in his right thigh. There was blood all over the floor and on Reaves' hands and up and down his pants leg.

"You son-of-a-bitch!" he screamed at me and pulled the tines of the fork out of his leg. He slipped the sweatshirt off, tied it around his thigh, then very slowly and very purposefully got back to his feet.

Jesus Christ! I said to myself and scrambled to my own feet and out the door into the cold, driving rain. The dirt pathway up the hillside had turned to mud. I slipped a couple of times as I clawed my way up it. Not looking back. Not daring to. Just racing toward the car before Norris Reaves could catch up to me again.

When I made it to the yard, I ran straight for the Pinto, jerked the door open, and dove across the seat for the gun rack. The Colt came away cold in my hand. I turned back to the hill just as Reaves was hobbling to the top—his leg all red and his chest and pants covered with mud.

"Don't come any closer, Reaves," I croaked at him.

He kept on coming, dragging his wounded leg behind him.

What the hell's keeping him up? I said to myself and raised both arms and aimed the pistol. But the gun barrel was wobbling badly and my head was still ringing from the punch I'd taken and, after all the adrenalin I'd been burning, I just didn't have any strength left. I squeezed the trigger and the gun barked, sending me tumbling back onto the car seat.

I'd missed him by a mile and I knew it. But like me, he was going on sheer nerve at that point. And after all the blood he'd lost, he just couldn't go any farther. He hobbled

147

into the yard, then pitched forward into the mud and lay there, panting out gray smoke and holding his bloody thigh with both hands.

That's how things stood for above five minutes. Reaves lying helplessly in the muddy yard and me sitting helplessly on the car seat. Both of us too drained of energy to move or to speak.

"Call an ambulance," he said after a time. "I'm going to bleed to death."

"Bleed to death," I said to myself and worked my way slowly out of the Pinto and up to the farmhouse porch. I sat down on the stairs, under the overhang, and stared at Reeves, who was lying beneath me in the muck.

"Call an ambulance, goddamn it!" he shouted.

"Where's Haskell Lord?" I said dully.

"I told you," he groaned. "I jus' don't know. Ain't it bad enough he brought the law down on me?"

"Where's your sister, then?"

He didn't say anything.

So I didn't move. I just sat there, listening to the rain on the roof, feeling my heart beat slow down again below the two hundred or so beats per minute it had been pumping back in the barn, and not thinking about how close I'd just come to death.

"Harrison," Reaves said suddenly. "Pop Warner's Trailer Park in Harrison. Now, won't you call an ambulance?"

I got to my feet and walked into the farmhouse.

17

THE INSIDE of the cabin smelled of sweat and dirty clothes. There were a couple of wooden chairs in the living room, an oil heater on the wall opposite the door, and a single photograph of an old man in a broken straw hat propped on a cabinet. The floors were painted wood, the walls unplastered lath. I walked through a bead curtain into the kitchen, found the phone on a trestle table beside a Franklin stove, and dialed the county police. Then I walked back into the living room and looked out the front window to make sure Norris hadn't gotten to his feet again. I had the pistol with me this time. Tucked in my belt. And if he did get up, I would have been only too happy to shoot him with it. But he was still lying in the yard.

There was only one other room in the tiny house. A bedroom to the left of the living room. I stepped inside and looked around. It was Norris's room. I had the feeling that it was Norris's house, too. There were muscle magazines scattered on a desk top and two posters of Franco Columbu on the walls. Jars of protein supplement on a bureau and in the top drawer a collection of just about every kind of vitamin I'd ever seen. But the second drawer and third one were a lot more interesting. Inside the second were two dozen big plastic jars of dexedrin. Twenty-four thousand hits of drugstore quality speed. And in the third drawer there were a couple of hundred glassine envelopes full of a white powder that was probably methedrine. That added up to a lot of barbells and chrome-plated wrenches. A tidy little business, indeed.

After I uncovered the cache of speed, I went through the whole room carefully and discovered several boxfuls of hospital syringes in the desk and about two thousand dollars in cash under a striped mattress on the floor. It was quite a haul. Not what I'd expected or what I'd been looking for, but it would certainly make the county cops happy. Once they saw it, I figured they wouldn't much care that I'd stuck old Norris in the thigh with a pitchfork.

I walked back out to the porch, sat down on the swing, and with Reaves groaning softly beneath me, waited for the county police to come calling.

It was nearly two o'clock when the troopers finished with me. They took my statement, confiscated the money and the drugs, and packed Norris off to the County Hospital, criminal wing. Everything went smoothly. I even got a slap on the back from one of the local detectives.

"Damn fine work!" he said. "Damn fine!"

Of course, my name wasn't going to appear officially in the record, he told me. But I didn't care about that. Just about getting off that muddy hillside as quickly as I could and down to the flats, where the world didn't come at you with a shovel handle.

He gave me directions back to the Pike. I probably could have gotten an escort if I'd wanted one. Once I hit the Pike, I pulled into a gas station; and while an old man in a Reds cap gassed up the Pinto, I walked back to the john and tried to clean up. I took one look at myself in the mirror and got the shakes. I could feel them coming on as soon as I got out of the car. They had to come, after that fracas in the barn. So I just sat down on the toilet seat and let them roll over me, in little waves of nausea and fright. Took deep breaths. Read my name off the credit cards in my wallet. Looked at the graffiti on the walls. And when I could stand up again without my knees buckling, washed my face and dabbed at my pants with a wet paper towel until I'd gotten most of the mud off of them. I couldn't do anything about the dark brown blood stains.

There was a small diner beside the service station. A stucco shack with a mansard roof and a yellow paper rack outside the door. I bought a paper even though I'd already read *The Enquirer* that morning with Kate, walked through the smoked glass door past the register lady, who looked as if she'd just come back from a funeral and was glad to be alive—prim, dark blue suit, with a huge carnation at the neck—and sat down at the lunch counter.

There was an old-fashioned chrome juke box on the

151

counter, the kind with metal tabs on the bottom attached to framed sheets inside a glass display. I flipped through the selections like I was flipping through the pages of a menu, shoved a quarter in the slot, and listened to some country music. After fifteen minutes of coffee and Loretta Lynn, I could think about what had happened on that hilltop without going numb inside. I'd come closer to death before. But not much closer. And a part of me knew that if Reaves had been a step quicker or a tad smarter I'd be lying under that barn floor, instead of sipping hot coffee and listening to Loretta Lynn and thinking about Kate Davis and about how nice it would be to hear her voice again. No matter how tough you think you are, Harry, I said to myself, how clever or quick or smart, what it comes down to in the end is luck, pure and simple. And I'd had it on my side that morning. Luck or Miss Moselle's stars and their baleful or benign influences. And, of course, the corollary was that there might come a time when I wouldn't be so lucky. That's why I was sitting there on that mushroom-shaped stool instead of driving off to find Pop Warner's Trailer Park. Which is what you should be doing, I told myself.

Around two-thirty, when the last lingering chill had left me and I felt safe and relatively lucky once again, I paid my chit, walked out to the Pinto, drove south to the expressway and then west to Ohio.

Pop Warner's Trailer Camp was located about ten miles up I-74 on the northern edge of Harrison township. There was a banner hung above the entranceway, decorated with Pop's name and a little picture of Pop in his prime, smiling out hopefully at a world of Air-streams and Winnebagos. Inside the gate, the place looked as grungy as a circus fairgrounds. Cigarette butts in the grass. Rusting tar barrels for the trash. A couple of plastic lawn chairs sitting in the mud, where they'd been left when the storm blew up. A dilapidated pickup truck jacked up on concrete blocks like third prize at a raffle. And maybe ten trailers scattered about a central yard. None in good repair. None of them hooked up to cars. This was the end of the line for those ten highway gypsies. This was home or something like it. The muddy pasture and the small concrete block house where old Pop probably held court and collected rents.

I parked the Pinto beside the block house, got out, and took a look around. There were clotheslines hanging between a couple of trailers. And somebody had planted a bed of mums in the dirt. But, all told, it was a pretty grim and unfriendly looking spot.

I was wondering which one of the trailers belonged to Effie Reaves when someone tapped me on the arm.

"Looking to buy, are you?" a cracked, cheerful voice asked me.

I turned around and saw an old man standing beside me, gazing out at the dingy lot with an unmistakable air of proprietorship. He was wearing a blue cardigan sweater over a coffee-stained undershirt and baggy chino pants. And he smelled strongly of whiskey and tobacco.

"You're Pop Warner," I said.

"That's me," he said and hiked up his pants with his thumbs. "I'm Pop, all right."

Pop had a fat, whiskey-red face, peppered on the cheeks and chin with razor stubble. It was the face on the banner fifteen years and two or three bankruptcies older. And while the mouth was still brimming with cheer, the weak blue eyes had the mean, disappointed look of a man who expects to be cheated.

"You need some gas, maybe?" he said, glancing at the Pinto. "I got a pump around back, if you do."

"No gas," I said. "But I could use some information."

"Directions, huh?" He looked over at the highway as if he'd had a hand in building it. "I can give you directions, all right. You headed for Indianapolis, are you?"

"I don't want directions, Pop," I said. "I want to know if you have a woman named Effie Reaves staying in your park."

He took a step back toward the block house and looked me up and down with shrewd reserve.

"I don't want no trouble, mister," he said.

I wondered if I looked like trouble or if Effie Reaves did.

"I don't want to cause any trouble, Pop. I just want to talk to the lady."

"Well, she ain't a big one for visitors," he said. "Not since that guy stopped hanging around."

"Medium height?" I said. "Black hair? Tattoo on his right forearm? Built like a weight-lifter?"

He rubbed his chin and said, "That's him, all right. All except for the weight-lifter part. This guy was pretty near skin and bones and real nervous acting."

This guy was on speed, I said to myself, and shivered when I thought of Norris Reaves. He'd claimed that Hack was a real Casey Jones. And the fact that he'd tried to kill me, rather than taking the chance that I couldn't find Hack or get him to talk, made me think that the last time Norris had seen him Hack must have been in very bad shape, indeed. A psychopathic killer was certainly scarey. But a psychopathic killer wigged out on speed was just about unthinkable. I sighed out loud and asked Pop Warner when he'd last seen Haskell Lord.

"Two, maybe three weeks now. She and him had a helluva fight. Shouting. Dishes breaking. I run a respectable place, mister, and I told her the next day I wouldn't stand for anymore of that. I think she got the message," he said with a wink. " 'Cause I ain't seen him around since then."

I had a sudden, nasty intuition. If in busting Norris Reaves I'd inadvertently busted Haskell Lord's drug connection, he was going to get mighty strung out and mighty mean in a few hours. Mean enough to kill again. And my girl Kate was out there somewhere, maybe with his intended victim.

"Which trailer does Effie live in?" I said to the old man.

"Oh, now, I don't know if . . . "

I dug into my wallet and pulled out a twenty and Pop Warner's face lit up like a Christmas tree light.

"Third one on your left from the front," he said and snatched the bill out of my hand.

He ambled back to the block house, snapping the twenty crisply between his fingers, and I walked across the muddy lot to the third trailer. It was a sixteen footer. All corrugated metal and about as squat and homey as a biscuit tin. There were some flowers in the tiny kitchen window beside the door and a yellow curtain drawn behind them. I pulled the screen open and knocked on the door.

No one answered. I waited a minute or so and knocked again. When there still wasn't any answer, I climbed the two metal steps that served as a stoop and tried the door handle. It was stuck. I put my weight against it and it opened a crack. Something was blocking it on the inside. Maybe a chair or a chock of wood. I wondered for a second whether Effie had been expecting unwelcome visitors like Hack or, maybe, like me, then I pushed again hard on the handle.

155

Blood dripped from beneath the door and down the two metal steps on to my shoes. I jumped off the stoop with a yelp of terror.

"Oh, my God," I said aloud.

Things were going too bad, too fast. Things that I couldn't anticipate or prepare for, and for a second I felt like running away. Instead I counted ten, took five deep breaths, and walked back up the metal steps—red now and greasy with the blood that was still seeping out from beneath the half-opened door. I hesitated a second before sticking my head inside.

It was dark in the trailer, except for the square of yellow light coming through the curtains in the kitchen window. But the smell was unmistakable. It was the smell of death. Violent death. I could hear a fly buzzing around and thought grimly that he was probably having a feast.

I took another deep breath and looked down at the floor, at the space behind the door. And my throat backed up.

I jerked the door shut and almost fell down the steps into the yard. Put a hand to the trailer, leaned over and vomited into the grass. I couldn't stop gagging for several minutes. Not since 'Nam, not since Khe Sanh. And even then, not like that . . . twisted thing, gouged and flayed almost past recognition. Parts cut away and piled like suet on the smoking floor.

Warner had come out of his block house and was walking toward me across the mud flat.

"Something wrong?" he called out. "You sick?"

Then he caught sight of the bloody steps and gasped.

"Call the police!" I shouted to him. "Now!"

He nodded and scampered back across the yard. I waited another couple of minutes, then followed him into the block house. When he finished talking to the cops, I phoned the library and told Miss Moselle, as calmly as I could, to get hold of Kate Davis and to tell her to come back to the library and to stay put until I returned.

They came with an ambulance. And two men in white hospital attendant's uniforms carried away what was left of Effie Reaves, sloshing like soup in a green disposal bag. A forensic team from the county police filed out the door as the ambulance drove off, while a beer-bellied deputy marshall from Harrison snapped pictures of the trailer. There were so many cops around, from so many different districts, that at first I didn't know who to talk to. A couple of them started squabbling about jurisdiction, then the beer-bellied marshall was chased away when it turned out he was off-duty and taking those snapshots to show his friends and neighbors.

Things settled down as soon as a white Buick Riviera pulled up and a huge, silver-haired man wearing a dark business suit and a Stetson stepped from behind the wheel. The decal on the door read *Hamilton County Sheriff*, and the strapping gent in the Stetson was Cal Levy.

A big ex-marine turned peace officer, Cal wore a Texas hat and carried a silver-plated .45 and had been county sheriff for as long as I could remember. Someone once told me that all it takes to become a county sheriff is part-ownership in a bowling alley and a bit of pull with the local branch of the Republican party. Well, Cal owned a whole bowling alley and a car dealership, to boot. But he was a dyed-in-the-wool Democrat, a party man who had actually worked, albeit with a scowl on his granite face, for George McGovern's election back in '72. Nobody held it against him, because, in spite of his politics, he was a damn good sheriff. And after all, how many Republicans in southern Ohio wear Stetsons and carry silver-plated revolvers?

He walked into the trailer and came back out a few minutes later, looking unnerved. Then one of the patrolmen pointed me out to him. Levy walked across the yard to where I was sitting on the stoop of Pop Warner's block house.

"Your name Stoner?" he said in a crusty, down-home voice.

I said I was Stoner.

He pushed the Stetson back from his forehead and looked over his shoulder at the Reaves trailer. The sun was setting in an orange band beneath the storm clouds. Yellow lamp light had begun to spill softly from the tiny kitchen window.

"Helluva thing," he said half to himself. "Never saw one like it before." He resettled the hat on his head and looked down at me. "I hear you discovered the body."

I nodded.

"I also hear you came looking for this woman and that you had a little run-in with her brother earlier in the day."

I told him all of it—about the books and about Twyla Belton and about Hack Lord, the man who'd turned that trailer into a charnel house. The man I'd come looking for.

"Brother," Cal Levy said. "You got a bitter job ahead of you, judging from what he did to that woman in there."

"I know it," I said. "The thing is he's on speed, and he might be so wigged-out he could kill again tonight."

"I'll put out an A.P.B. on him right away," Levy said. "That tattoo on his arm ought to be easy enough to spot."

"It hasn't been so far," I said gloomily.

He grunted. "At least it's a starting point."

"Do you know the time of death? " I asked him. "Or how he got into the trailer without being seen?"

158

"Let's go see what the lab team's got to say."

We walked back across the yard, which had dried into furrows in the cold evening air, and up to the door of the trailer. I hesitated a second before gripping the handle, then jerked it open.

They'd cleaned up most of the blood and waste. All that was left to show that Effie Reaves had been butchered on the trailer floor was a chalk outline behind the door, shaped vaguely like a human body. I hadn't really seen the inside of the trailer before; so while Levy talked to his forensic officer, I took a look around. The front door opened on a small living room, decorated with cheap pine furniture stained chocolate brown. There was a couch on the right wall and an arm chair opposite it and a coffee table between them. The table and chair had been overturned; the chair cushions were stained with blood. Beyond the living room area was the kitchen—just a plank breakfast table, a couple of canvas chairs and an L.P. range. The table was lying on its side and there was a large blood stain on the straw mat beneath it. The door to the bedroom was closed. It must have started in the kitchen, I thought, while they were sitting at the table. Then they'd worked their way forward to the living room, until she'd gone down behind the door and he'd pounced on her.

"She'd been dead almost two hours when you found her," Levy said to me. "It happened in the thick of that rain storm we had. Old man Warner says he didn't stick his head outside his hut until after it cleared up. And then he's a juicer anyway. Your boy Lord must have walked up to the front door during the storm. She let him in and then they sat down at the table in the kitchen. He used some kind of razor in case you wondered. Cut off one of her hands with it. We also found a breadknife stuck inside the body.

159

Got it bagged over there if you want to take a look."

I shook my head.

"Don't blame you. Anyway he did his business, then went out through the bedroom window after he got through. There's a rest stop on the other side of this pasture. We figured he might have had a car stashed over there. Just walked across the field, cut her up, then walked back again the way he came. Nobody in any of the other trailers seen a thing. But they were probably glued to their radios. We had a twister come through Xenia one October killed several people. Folks living in trailers always keep that sort of thing in mind. The lab team found some pills in the bedroom. Dexedrine."

I looked at him and said, "I'm surprised he didn't take them with him."

"He could have taken a handful," Levy said. "The jar's half-empty, so there's no telling who took what. They also found a high school yearbook back there, lying open on the bed. 1973. Withrow. Couldn't have been the woman's, so it might have belonged to your boy. And there's a painting on the wall in there with his initials on it—H.L."

"Could I take a look?" I said.

"Sure."

We edged past the forensic men, who were packing up their evidence kits, past the overturned kitchen table, and through the door into the bedroom at the rear of the trailer. Cal Levy flipped on the overhead light. There was a small mirrored bureau on the left wall and a double bed on the right. The window that Haskell had used to make his escape was set beside the bed.

"Picture on the south wall," Levy said, reading from a notepad. He pointed to the rear wall of the trailer.

It was a watercolor sketch of the Overlook, framed and

160

matted by an expert hand. Everything was spongy and melting in the drawing—the trees, the bridge, the statue—like an Oldenberg sculpture, as if the world, as Hack Lord saw it, was just so much wax held too close to a fire. Maybe the fire inside his own violent mind. It gave me a chill to look at it and then to look at the bed and to think that that's what must have been in his head as he lay there beside Effie Reaves.

A girl with a face like a child's drawing of mother, that's what Aamons had said. Another woman who had, in fact, been old enough to be his mother—a death-mother who had fed him drugs and God only knew what kind of twisted love. Neat symmetry, like the two drawings of the Overlook. So neat, it unnerved me.

"Where's the yearbook?" I said.

Levy glanced at his notes. "They put it on the bureau."

I walked over to the bureau and examined it.

It was Haskell's, all right. And it was open to the page of his senior picture. He'd had a bull neck even then. Coal black hair and those heavy-lidded eyes. He looked young and tough and handsome in that picture. But that was before the tattoo and the speed and Effie Reaves.

I flipped to the rear of the yearbook and found him again, looking tough in the front row of the wrestling team picture. And again, paradoxically, in an art club photograph. Still looking tough. He'd been a complicated boy. A true Capricorn, as Miss Moselle had described him.

I looked again at the picture on the wall. Benson Howell had said that Hack and his kind wanted to be caught, that that was why they left clues and sent notes to the police. And the drawing and the yearbook picture were certainly giveaways to anyone who could read their meaning. He'd signed his name to each and, by means of the drawing, marked a path that could be traced to Twyla Belton. In fact, he'd been leaving a trail of evidence behind him for better than two years—a trail that had been lying cold until I happened across it. It had been an accident on my part, a concatenation of my own instincts and Kate's dogged research and a good deal of luck. But I *had* found the trail and, in some irrational way, I'd begun to feel responsible for it and for him, as if I'd been chosen "it" in a game far older and more grave than hide-and-seek. It was up to me now. Somehow, I felt I knew that and felt, as well, that he was out there, somewhere in the night, waiting almost eagerly to learn whether I had the skill to match him move for move.

18

THEY WERE waiting for me when I got back to the library at half-past nine that night. Miss Moselle and her gray-haired friends in their dowdy print dresses and high-topped shoes. Leon Ringold, sitting in one of those orange chairs with his feet barely skimming the rug and a look of smug impatience on his face. And, of course, my girl Kate. Best of all, my girl Kate. Who came rushing around the circulation counter to greet me as I came through the door.

I gave her a big hug and whispered, "God, I'm glad to see you."

"Me, too," she said and kissed me on the lips.

I looked over her shoulder. "Why the reception?"

"They were worried about you, Harry," she said under her breath. "Miss Moselle heard about Effie Reaves's murder on the news and they decided to stay here until they found out if you were all right. Even Leon."

"I'm touched," I said. And meant it.

I looked over her shoulder again at that odd crew of little old ladies and grinned. They'd smiled as one when I'd come through the door. And when Kate had run up to me, they'd turned away as one and started sorting through catalogue cards and stamping overdue books. It was low-grade sentimental comedy, but damn sweet and satisfying.

"I'm all right," I proclaimed to one and all. "And thanks for worrying."

"I must say Harold," Miss Moselle said without looking up from her pile of index cards. "You lead an exciting life. Perhaps a little too exciting?"

"After today," I said, "I think I might agree with you."

It was like a family gathering. All of us sitting around one of those huge varnished oak tables, sipping tepid coffee and discussing what we were going to do about the family problem. Because that's what Haskell Lord had become to them —a family problem.

I hadn't wanted it that way. But what are you going to do? I asked myself, as I sat there planning strategy with seven old ladies and a fubsy little man with the well-scrubbed face of a freshman advisor. They were involved whether I'd wanted them to be or not. They'd been involved from the start, working through whatever grapevine they'd established over the years. They'd known before I did why Ringold wanted to hire me. They'd known about Leo Sachs and about Twyla Belton. And now about Haskell Lord and Effie Reaves. Picked it up and transmitted it to one another the way plants are said to transmit the slightest vibrations. A kind of Brownian movement of gossip and rumor that was impossible to defeat. So I quit trying to fight it and accepted the fact that, whether I liked it or not, my little old ladies were involved in the case.

I gave them a bowdlerized account of what had gone on that day, from Norris Reaves Auto Repair Shop to Pop Warner's Trailer Park. And they took it all, murder and mayhem, with a stoic calm. That surprised me a bit, although at that point I don't know why I should have been surprised. Those seven old ladies were probably tougher than, say, your average professional football team. And Jessie Moselle was the toughest of the lot.

"We're all librarians here, Harold," she said when I'd finished telling them about what I'd found in the Reaves woman's trailer. "We haven't seen much of life, outside of what a few great minds have written about it. And certainly nothing as terrible as what you've described. But I think there is a certain courage that comes with education, don't you? Not a physical courage, like your own. But an intellectual one. And it is our library and our patrons that this man has been preying on. I don't think any of us will tolerate that."

"No, indeed," another old lady said.

"So we want to help," Jessie Moselle said. "In any way we can. After what you've told us, I'm not so sure that Haskell Lord himself wouldn't want us to help you stop him."

"It seems odd to me," Leon Ringold said, "that he would have killed this older woman. After the Belton girl I would have expected someone younger."

"I don't think he's through, yet, Leon," Jessie said daintily.

165

Ringold blanched. "You're not serious?"

"I'm afraid she is," I said. "The Reaves killing simply doesn't fit the pattern we've been developing with the books. The whole motive for killing younger women like Twyla was to deflect the sexual and emotional rage Lord felt for the older ones like Effie Reaves and his mother. To kill them instead of committing matricide. I think we have to look upon what happened this afternoon as an unplanned homicide. Either Haskell Lord was so stoned on speed that he lost his mind entirely, or something the Reaves woman said or did pushed him over the edge. According to Pop Warner, the guy who runs the trailer park, they'd had a bad fight two weeks ago and Effie'd thrown Haskell out. Maybe that's what triggered it."

"So the defaced art books have nothing to do with Ms. Reaves?" Ringold said. "She was not his intended victim?"

"I don't think she was," I said. "But I wouldn't say that the books had nothing to do with her. Judging from the sketch that was found in the trailer, Haskell was apparently something of an artist himself before he met Effie Reaves a couple of years ago. And he was a body-builder, too. After he got hooked on speed and on Effie, I'm guessing that both skills went down the drain. Since the pictures he cut up were a sort of melding of physical and artistic excellence, it's possible that cutting them up and cutting up Twyla Belton was Haskell's way of getting back at the Reaves woman and at his mother for what they'd done to him."

"Like Samson and Delilah," Miss Moselle said.

"And now that he's killed her," Ringold said. "What can we expect?"

I shook my head and said, "I honestly don't know."

Nobody said anything for a moment.

"What are the police doing about this!" Ringold said nervously. "Shouldn't we have some protection here at the library?"

"They've got an A.P.B. put on Haskell in the city and in the county," I said. "But you may be right. It might not be a bad idea to get some police protection for the ladies here at the library. He has to be feeling an enormous guilt for killing Effie Reaves—that is, if he's feeling anything at all. My guess is he's going to find someone to blame it on. And in his state I just don't know who that will be."

"I think it would be selfish to make the police guard our library," Miss Moselle said. "We must look after ourselves. And allow the officers to concentrate on searching for this man."

Ringold looked at her the way he'd looked at his office door on Monday morning, with a kind of hapless, disgusted resignation. He was licked and he knew it.

"We shall hold the fort, Harold," Jessie Moselle said stoutly. "Have no fear of that. And you must go out and find this fellow and stop him."

Kate Davis had been uncharacteristically quiet during our round-table discussion. When we got out to the parking lot, I asked her why.

"You've had a pretty hard day, Harry," she said. "Are you sure you want to hear it?"

"I guess that depends on what *it* is."

We got into the car and when she didn't say anything for a long moment, I started to worry. Kate was not a secret-keeper. At least, she didn't keep them for long. It went against her own liberated code of honor. Everything on the surface, everything out in the open. Even the uncertainties and the unanswerables. The things that my generation of lovers usually slid past with a smile or a kiss, the way we slide past the forgotten words of an old song. So if she were keeping quiet, it had to be for a fairly good reason—something she wanted to spare me or didn't want to admit to herself after that dreadful, violent day.

"What is it, Kate?" I said. "What do you want to say?"

She scrunched down on the car seat, pulled her coat around her neck, and propped her knees on the dash. "I did some research of my own on our six ladies today. And I'm stumped. A couple of them look vaguely like Twyla. And all of them are interested in art—that's why they took the books out in the first place. What I need is a solid clue. Some indisputable link between Haskell and the girls. But I don't know what it is. I guess that's part of what's bothering me. I guess I'm frustrated. The police are keeping an eye on all six girls just in case."

"That's good," I said.

"After I finished with my ladies, I started thinking about what Howell told you, so I went up to Withrow to talk with Hack's teachers. He was a pretty scarey fellow, all right. Even in high school. More interesting, though, is what the assistant principal, a man named Rogers, told me. I only talked to him for a minute — he had a meeting to go to — but he said that Hack's been seen hanging around the Withrow gym and track."

"Recently?" I said.

"Right up until a couple of weeks ago."

"That *is* interesting," I said half to myself. Withrow was only a stone's throw from the Lord home—close enough for a family visit. In fact, after being kicked out by Effie

Reaves, Hack might not have had anywhere else to go but home. Of course, that would mean that Jake or his mother or both of them had been lying to me about not having seen Hack in better than two years. An innocent enough lie, to be sure. But a lie. I decided to take another look at the Lord home in the morning and, perhaps, do a bit of research on Mother Lord and her polite son. It wouldn't hurt to check in with Gerald Arnold, either. A man who knew a good deal about speed freaks and where they hung out.

"Rogers said that Hack looked like death itself," Kate said suddenly. "Terrible hollows under his eyes. Emaciated. Extremely nervous."

"He's a speed freak, Kate."

"I know," she said.

I looked at her face. Her blue eyes looked stunned and fearful. And I realized all at once that *that* was what she'd been holding back—the terrible fact that she could be as scared as I'd been in that barn or when I leaped off the metal stoop of Effie Reaves's trailer. She was terrified and she didn't want to admit it.

"Bad day, huh?" I said.

She nodded. "I know it sounds stupid. I know it's just a racket that I'm playing with my child. But when I heard about what happened to the Reaves woman, I guess I realized that Haskell Lord was a pretty dangerous man."

"Came as a surprise, did it?"

She made a face at me. "You're being a critical parent again," she said and didn't sound amused. "Look we all have our own ways of adapting to stress. I tend to sulk, that's all. To withdraw. That's all it is, Kate." She slapped herself on the thigh. "You're just behaving like an adapted child."

Sometimes I think that the chief problem with psychotherapy is that it teaches us to regard all feelings as problematical. I didn't tell Kate that. But I did tell her how I'd felt when I was sitting on the john in that service station—too scared to move or to think.

"Well you had a good reason to be frightened," she said.

"While you, Kate Davis, girl detective, don't?"

She made another face. "All right, so I'm scared. Does that make you feel better?"

I pulled her to me and she laid her head on my chest.

"We'll get him, Kate," I said. "We'll get him. I promise you."

She laughed spiritlessly. "Promise?" she said. "You're a born rescuer, Harry."

"That doesn't sound so hot," I said.

She laughed again, this time with pleasure, and kissed me on the lips. "In your case, it's terrific."

Late that night, with the wind shaking the windows and a little music playing faintly on the Globemaster, we made love. Not furiously, as we had the night before. But gently, slowly, as if we were both acknowledging what that day had cost us in energy, as if we were both being a little tender, a little solicitous of our wounds and weaknesses.

It wasn't as raw and exciting as it had been the night before. But it was sweeter. I knew when we'd finished and she was lying in my arms, her hair damp and her breath warm on my chest, that I was falling in love with her. It was ludicrous after all of her talk, after all of the warnings she'd been giving out. Still I could feel it inside me like an afterglow. Not just a sexual satisfaction but a gratitude, if that's the word. A pleasure in her pleasure and in her presence.

170

In her face and in her body and in what she had done for me.

Kate Davis, I said to myself.

I held her tightly, cupping her breast in my hand and listening to the sound of her breathing as it slowed into sleep. And then I was asleep, too. And that terrible day was finally over.

19

SHE WAS up before I was on that Friday morning. Fixing eggs and bacon in the little cubicle that the realty company calls a kitchen. Humming old songs. And just generally acting spry and domestic. At eight-thirty, she popped her head through the bedroom door and announced that breakfast was served. Then she served it. On a black tray that I used to hold a couple of potted geraniums. The eggs smelled like geraniums and potting soil. We dined *au naturel.* And when we finished, I rolled over on the blanket and ran my fingertip across her breasts and down that flat, downy belly. Her eyes grew soft and she wrapped her arms around my shoulders and pulled me on top of her.

"You know this could get to be a habit," she said.

She ran her hand down *my* belly.

Then there wasn't any sound but the Globemaster and the soughing of the mattress springs and the sounds of our lovemaking.

"I used to live in an apartment on Ohio Avenue," Kate said, as we lay together afterward watching the sunlight spill through the bedroom windows. "It was right after my divorce and I was all bent out of shape and terribly unhappy. This was a big apartment, with fifteen-foot ceilings and no soundproofing. Every noise that the neighbors made washed through it like the sounds of a sea. Have you ever read *The Enormous Radio*? That's what it was like. I heard all the squabbling and cursing, all the bickering that I'd lived with for three years. All the ways Ed and I had failed before I lost my nerve and left him. And it weighed on me, Harry, because I was really in love with him. Married fresh out of high school. Sweethearts at the ripe age of eighteen. My God, there can't be love that's much more intense than that.

"Anyway, I was sinking. Alone in that cave with all those voices battering at each other. And then, one night, I heard the creak of a bedspring from upstairs. You know, the old-fashioned kind of bedsprings that look like something you might distill liquor with? And it squeaked and it squeaked, until I realized that whoever was living above me was making love. After awhile I stopped listening and started wondering who it was up there making the noise. Because he had a real nice sense of rhythm. Now slow. And then so fast the springs started to sing like a tea kettle."

I tousled her hair. "Did you ever find out who it was?"

"One night I went up there and knocked on the door. He

173

wasn't good-looking, it turned out. Skinny with a beard and dark, soulful eyes. But I was enchanted by the sound of those bedsprings. I honestly think they were what brought me back to life. Plus a little help from my shrink. I didn't waste any time. When you're just starting therapy you don't, you know. If you think I'm impetuous now, you should have seen me then. I was as devoted to candor as a high school valedictorian. No more holding things in for Kate. All sunny surface and uninhibited instincts. I was a real asshole. That's step one in therapy, Harry. The asshole stage. So I said to the guy, 'I live downstairs and I'd like to make love to you.' His eyes got as big as gumballs. 'Sure thing,' he said. Then I told him it was only for that once, that I wasn't looking to become involved, just to gratify a whim. Because I'd spent a long time not gratifying whims. He licked his chops and said, 'Sure thing.' So we made love. And you wouldn't have believed it, but it was really wonderful, lying there and listening to those bedsprings sigh and sing."

Kate laughed at herself. "Stupid story, huh?"

"No," I said.

She looked a little embarrassed. After all, she was the girl who thought the past was sad and small, as if real life were invariably huge and happy. So I told her one of my own misadventures. Told her about Jo Riley, the black-haired lady with the heart-shaped face, whom I'd loved and lost. And about the nights I'd spent after she was gone, trying to convince myself and everyone else that it was still O.K. with old Harry. Mornings when I'd get out of bed and, maybe a half hour later, the girl who I'd picked up in some bar would get up, too. Only there wasn't any breakfast in bed in those days. Just some small, sad silences while we dressed. And a kiss at the door that was as personal as a handshake. And when she'd gone, I'd go into the bathroom and count the circles under my eyes like I was counting the rings on a tree trunk. And it would always come up the same sad, small number. That kind of addition only has one sum. And it's depressing.

"You never found her?" Kate said. "You never found Jo?"

"No," I said. "Which is funny. Because that's my business, finding things that people have lost and want back."

She propped herself on an elbow and looked at me sympathetically. "She was a fool," Kate said.

I laughed at her. "Well she didn't have your fine sense of my virtues. She didn't have the heart for this kind of life."

Kate sat back in the bed. "In spite of what I said last night, I *do*. And I'm going to prove it to you."

"And how do you plan to do that?" I asked.

"By helping to catch the Ripper," she vowed solemnly.

We got dressed and around ten o'clock we walked out to the parking lot.

"Where are we going?" Kate said in a chipper voice.

I thought over that "we" for a second and decided, why not?

"First to the Lord house. Then to an old friend of mine who knows a bit about speed freaks and where they hang out."

"All right," Kate said. "Lead on."

We took Taft to the expressway, got off at Dana, then went north on Madison to Stettinius. I pulled up in front of the Lord home at ten-thirty. After filling Kate in on what we could expect from the mother and from the loyal brother, we hopped out of the car and walked up the cut-

175

stone pathway to the front door. The maple trees along the street had been stripped bare by the storm, and that sweet anise-smell of goldenrod was almost gone. It felt like winter on the street—a bright blue cold that should have gone with snow and the rigors of December, not with the burnt-orange of an October morning.

With Kate beside me, I walked up to the stoop and rang the doorbell.

Jake answered again, in another turtle-neck sweater and loose khaki pants, with a look of exhaustion on his tow-headed, choir-boy's face. I realized that the police had probably paid the Lords a call the night before, after I'd talked with Al Foster. And hearing the bitter truth about his brother, hearing what he was wanted for, could easily have made for a sleepless night.

"Mr. Stoner," he said with a trace of bitterness in his voice. "What more can we do for you?"

"I wonder if we could come in, Jake, and talk?"

"About Haskell, you mean?"

I nodded.

He took a deep breath and said, "Why not? Mother isn't in any state to talk. Well, you can imagine. But if you want to talk to me. I mean if there's anything . . ."

He looked down miserably at the walk.

Kate patted him on the arm and Jake flinched and pulled back.

"I'm sorry," he said after a second. "It's just been an awful night. And then I've never much liked being touched. I guess it's a Lord family tradition."

He led us down that corridor to the fifties den, where we sat on the L-shaped couch. I introduced him to Kate and he nodded to her politely. Then I told him what I knew

176

about his brother. About the speed. About the art books and the killings and the fact that Hack had been seen at the Withrow gym.

"I know it's a hard thing to ask of you, Jake. I know how you feel about your brother. But Withrow's only a stone's throw from here. Have you seen him since he moved away? Has he come by the house?"

Jake glanced about the room with the same forlorn look he'd had on his face when he'd heard his mother talking Haskell down. He shook his head sadly and said, "Yeah, I've seen him. Or what was left of him. I just didn't want Mother to know."

"When was the last time you saw him?"

"A couple of months ago."

"Do you know why he was hanging around the gym and the field house?" I said. "What drew him back there?"

"Old times, I guess," Jake said with a sigh. "I guess he just couldn't believe what had happened to him."

I looked closely at the boy's face. "You don't know where he is now, do you, Jake?"

He didn't bat an eye. "No. I'd tell you if I did." Jake got up suddenly from his chair. "Can I show you something, Mr. Stoner? Can I show you what Hack used to be like? Then maybe you'll understand why he came back to the school and the house."

He led us back down the hallway, up the mahogany staircase to a second floor room. "This was Hack's room," he said as we stood outside the door. "His stuff is still inside."

He pushed the door open and we walked in.

At first glance it looked like a boy's room out of a television serial, right down to the Dartmouth pennant hung

177

above the knotty pine bunkbeds and the trophies on the bureau. Only when you looked at it more carefully, the rah-rah flavor disappeared. Instead of black-light posters and a picture of Farrah Fawcett, you saw Haskell's water colors on the walls, matted and neatly framed like the one in Effie Reaves's trailer. Instead of *Time* and *Newsweek* there were wrestling magazines piled in a wicker basket. A family Bible sat on a lamp table, with a red ribbon sticking out of the gold leaves to mark the page. A sketch of Jesus was pasted to the closet door, His eyes looking empty and remote, as if He'd lost all interest in the inhabitants of that little room. And above the bunk beds, a single photo of Haskell and Jake, comparing biceps while their mother looked on with mixed approval—a little allegory of Lord family life.

It was all as sad as Jacob had known it would be, full of the heart-breaking ironies that define any tragic scene. The paintings, sensitive and colorful, dwindling to that bare line sketch of a remorseless Christ on the closet door. The Bible with its tatter of ribbon and its birthday cake trim, sitting on the bedstand as if that was what he'd read before sleep —searching out some reason for his own fitful, violent turn of mind. And all of it set in that never-never land of the college banners and the gilded trophies, which sat like bronzed baby shoes on the pine bureau.

"If you could have seen him before the Reaves woman," Jake said. "Before she and mother had destroyed his confidence, you'd understand why I love him. He was so talented, Mr. Stoner. So sensitive and so strong. He was perfect." Jake blushed as if he'd said a dirty word. "I know that sounds corny, but he was very important to me. I wouldn't have survived childhood without him. Without my big brother."

Jake lowered his head. "I'll let you know if he comes back, Mr. Stoner. But I hope he doesn't. God help me, I hope you never find him. And that wherever he is, he's found peace."

We left Jacob in his brother's room and walked back down the staircase to the door.

"It's so sad," Kate said to me. "And terrible. I don't know how he can stand it."

"That wasn't Haskell Lord we were seeing in there," I said to her. "That was Jake. The way he remembers his brother. And that is sad. But so is what his brother did to Twyla Belton and Effie Reaves. And more terrible than you could believe."

"I just feel sorry for him," she said. "That's all."

We drove silently through the cold autumn morning to Ogden Street, parked in front of the elm with the yellow X on its trunk, and walked up that dingy stairway to the third floor, to Gerald Arnold's hippie flat.

"Who lives here?" Kate said, eyeing the peace symbol and the cross on the door. "Bishop Pike?"

"Gerald Arnold," I said flatly. "A man who knows a bit about speed."

I knocked at the door and waited. If he was coming off the night shift it would take him a moment to wake up and get his bearings. But Gerald didn't take that moment. He just flung the door wide open and said, "Yeah?"

He was naked as a jay, except for a sweater cap on his hairy head and a joint he'd filed like a pencil behind his ear and apparently forgotten when he'd gone to sleep.

Kate clapped a hand to her mouth and laughed. Gerald looked down penitently at his naked body. "Oh, wow, man!" he said. "I'm sorry!"

He padded over to the mattress, pulled off the sheet, and wrapped it around his hips.

"I don't know what's come over me," he said, knotting the sheet at his waist. "I've been doing some weird things lately, man. Forgetting where I am and stuff. It's that fucking night shift, you know?" He looked down at the floor and said, "And then going to church all the time. It just wears you down, man."

"Can we come in, Gerald?"

"Oh, sure, man," he said and sat down on the mattress. "Just don't pay any attention to the mess."

The place looked exactly the same as it had on Wednesday night. Right down to the calico cat lapping milk from a saucer. I sat down on one of the Heart Mart armchairs and Kate looked at the other one and said, "I'll pass."

"So what can I do for you?" Gerald Arnold said.

"If I wanted to buy some speed, Gerald, where could I get it?"

"I'm clean, man," he said quickly. "I told you I'm clean."

"This is purely academic, Gerald. I just want to know who deals speed in Hyde Park and where I can find them."

"Academic, huh? That means not-for-real, right?"

I laughed.

He scratched his head, found the joint, blushed a little, then said, "Aw, well, what the hell!" and lit up. "You do a little smoke, man?" he said, passing the joint to me.

I shook my head. "Different generation."

"Well, I'm not!" Kate said.

"All right!" Gerald passed her the j and she took a long toke.

"It ain't real good stuff," Gerald said. "But it'll get you high."

Kate blew out the smoke and grinned at him. "This is dynamite!"

"No," he said with a tickle of pride in his voice. "It's just street-grass." He took another toke and passed it back to Kate, who was beginning to look a little glassy-eyed.

"About the speed," he said and puffed out a cloud of sweet-smelling smoke. "There was a dude selling pills up near the high school. Real ragged-looking fucker with mean eyes and black hair."

"I think I know him," I said grimly and thought that old Hack hadn't been hanging around that gym for sentimental reasons alone. "Where would you find this guy, if you wanted to score some drugs?"

He shrugged. "Up at the track, man. There are some trees behind the fieldhouse and he'd kind of mosey on back there to do his business. Only I ain't seen this guy around in awhile."

"How long a while?"

"At least a couple of weeks, man. And that's an eternity in the trade."

I glanced at Kate, who was now sitting in the other chair and looking very happy.

"Is there another place in Hyde Park where speed freaks hang out? Some place where they might know this guy or what happened to him?"

"Yeah," he said. "There's a place in Oakley on Edwards Road. A coffee shop, you know? Some dudes over there used to hang out with this guy. Only . . ." He looked at Kate and shook his head. "I wouldn't be taking no chick over there. Especially a nice chick like her. Dudes might get the wrong idea, you know?"

"Will you come over there with me, Gerald?" I said,

181

because I had the feeling that I wouldn't get anywhere on my own. "All I want to know is where the guy you've been talking about hangs out."

"Sure," he said. "I'll go. But it'll cost you."

I reached for my wallet and Gerald shook his head.

"You gotta come to church with me, man. Talk to Brother Stearns. Get a little religion, man."

I smiled and told him I'd go to church with him.

20

KATE WASN'T thrilled with the idea of splitting up. And it didn't take a detective to figure out why. She was still feeling guilty about the previous night and she didn't want to leave me with the impression that there was a drop of fear left in her body. For better than three years, she hadn't wanted to leave anyone with that impression, because for better than three years she'd been secretly afraid that it was her weakness, rather than her strength, that had cost her her marriage.

"This is a pretty lousy thing to do to your partner, Harry," she said as we pulled into the library lot.

I pointed to the back seat, where Gerald Arnold was

bouncing around like a kid on a merry-go-round horse, and said, "It wasn't my idea. It was Gerald's."

"Yeah?" She gave me a look, as if to say, "You didn't put up much of a fight." And of course, I hadn't. Whether it stung her pride or not, I didn't want Kate involved with the men Gerald and I were going to meet. I wanted her out of harm's way, even if it meant cheating on our agreement. Which was hopelessly old-fashioned and chauvinistic and probably a few other disagreeable things. But that's the way I felt.

"Well, thanks for the grass, Gerald," Kate said as she got out of the car. "And try to see that this one doesn't get into any trouble."

"Oh, I'll look out for him," he said earnestly.

"I'll be back in about an hour," I told her. "If I come up with anything, I'll call. If not, I'll probably stop at Withrow to see if I can dig up any more information about Hack."

"Uh-huh," she said grouchily and walked off to the library door. Gerald tapped me on the shoulder.

"Yeah?" I said.

"I was just wondering," he said in all innocence. "What does a housing inspector have to do with speed freaks?"

I laughed. "I'm a private detective, Gerald. Not a housing inspector."

"Oh!" He smiled as if that had taken care of all his doubts. "Like Rockford Files, huh?"

"Like Rockford Files," I said.

"Neat," Gerald Arnold said and sat back on the seat.

Oakley is a small municipality on the northeast side of town. It's a blue-collar neighborhood, for the most part—modest homes that are as decent as well-kept graves and, here and there, a small factory or block of retail stores. Like most blue-collar neighborhoods, it has its rough spots. Bars where the boys that work at G.M. and Cincinnati Millacron go to blow off a little steam. The part of Edwards Road that Gerald directed me to was very rough, indeed. Right above old Duck Creek Road. A hillside dotted with tough saloons and eateries, full of truckers and motorcycle hoods.

We parked beneath a drooping street lamp on the west side of Edwards, and Gerald told me to wait in the car while he checked things out.

He walked across the street to one of the diners—a seedy-looking spot called the Tic-Toc Lounge. *Real Home Cooking,* it said in decal on the window. But the two or three guys sitting side-saddle on their choppers in the parking lot didn't look as if they knew what a real home was. Or much cared. Gerald walked up to one of them and started to talk. He pointed across Edwards to where I was parked. The guy he was talking to held out his hand as if he were expecting a tip.

I figured that's exactly what he *was* expecting. And I was right. Gerald came trotting back across the street and leaned up against the Pinto. "He'll talk to you," he said. "But he wants some bread."

"How much bread?" I said.

"Twenty bucks."

I said all right.

Gerald waved his arm and a skinny, balding man hopped off one of the bikes and crossed the street. He had a head like a painted egg. Little curls of brown hair that lay flat against his naked skull. Big brown eyes that were almost boyish, in spite of the dark circles beneath them. A small chipmunk's mouth full of black broken teeth that looked as if they'd been knocked out, once upon a time, and then thrown back inside for storage. He was wearing a leather

185

motorcycle jacket, blue jeans, and sneakers. No shirt. And he smelled like Norris Reaves's goat shed. Speed breath. The smell of rot.

"What's happening, man?" he said when he got up to the car. He sat down on the front seat beside me, and Gerald leaned against the open window next to him. This guy had a squeaky voice and it came out in quick, nervous bleats, like the chirping of a baby doll that someone kept stepping on out of spite. "You got the bread, man?"

He held out his hand—an old man's hand, hooked and grimy with a couple of nailess fingers, like a hand in a horror film. I began to understand why Jake Lord had wanted to show me that boyhood room, to show me what his brother had been like before Effie Reaves and the drugs had destroyed him. It was as if Haskell Lord were sitting there beside me. This grim biker was probably no older than Haskell, and like Hack, he was burned out—all of the history that's packed inside of us, that gives us form and character, had been let out through the holes in his arm. What was left was that eggshell head and the hunger that made his fingers twitch expectantly.

I gave him twenty bucks and he folded it up neatly and stuck it in the top of his sock.

"All right," he said. "What do you want to hear?"

"Do you know Haskell Lord?" I said.

"Yeah, I know Hack. Very weird dude. Very weird."

I wondered for a second what on earth constituted "weird" in the world he lived in.

"Have you seen him around?"

"Not in two weeks," he said. "Oh, man, he was in very bad shape. Very bad. Got kicked out by his old lady, you know? Weird old lady, too, man. Real hard case. She used to dole the shit out to him a little at a time. He'd have to do things for it, you know? Like ream her? Grossed me out."

I felt a little sick. "You know where he is now?"

"Ask his brother, man," the biker said.

"Jake?"

"Sure, man. He went everywhere with Hack. Like his shadow, man. Followed him wherever he'd go, you know? Man, that kid *loves* his brother!"

"How did Hack feel about it?" I said.

The biker shrugged. "How'd you feel, man, if some wimp was always hanging around with you, telling you to shape up and crying about the good old days and warning you to quit your evil ways before God got you? Man, he hated his fucking guts."

"Are you sure?" I said.

The biker sat back in the car seat and eyed me as if I were inalterably square. "It's like this, man," he said. "Some guy I used to know in high school, man, I see him every now and then in the streets, you know? And he always gets this fucked-up look on his face, man. Like he can't believe it's me and he's so damn sorry and all. You dig what I'm saying? I mean the only reason he's glad to see me is because seeing me gets him off. He spends the rest of the day just shaking his head and telling himself how hard life is. But, man, he ain't seein' me. He's just seein' some part of the past, man, some part of himself that he don't like to think about. I'm just his excuse to feel glad he ain't like me. Now I hate that dude, man. Wouldn't you?"

I didn't answer him. I was too busy thinking over what he'd said about Jake and Hack. Not the love-hate business, which was predictable given their straight-laced upbringing and the fact that Hack had fallen off so completely from what he once had been. Benson Howell had said that the

Ripper would have a grotesquely ambivalent relationship with his siblings, so that part was no surprise. It was the other thing, the business about Jake following Hack wherever he went, that had me worried. If it were true—and I didn't know how much credence to give to what the biker had told me, since he was so obviously speaking for himself as well as for Hack—then Jake might not have been telling me the truth when he said that he hadn't seen his brother in over two months. If he was in the habit of following Hack around, it was just possible that Jake knew where Hack was at that moment. He could be covering for him, all right. After watching his brother degenerate into something like what was sitting on the seat beside me, he'd have an awful good reason for lying. That is, *if* the biker were telling me the truth. What I needed was some more reliable testimony about Hack and his brother. And I knew where to get it.

I looked back at the biker, who was staring at me as if I were Dad's wallet left out on the bedroom dresser, and said, "I guess that's it. Thanks for the help."

He didn't budge. "I think I should get paid more money, man. I deserve it—all the shit I told you."

"You got your money," I said to him. "Now get out of here."

He snorted and turned a bit on the car seat. I turned, too, so that I was facing him. There wasn't enough room for either of us to throw a good punch, if it came to that. But squared around I could use both arms to tie him up if he pulled a knife or a razor.

"Tough guy!" the biker sneered and reached into his coat pocket.

I lunged forward. But before I could grab his hand, Gerald Arnold had reached through the side window and thrown his right arm around the biker's neck.

"Cut it out, Lester," he said, right into the guy's ear. "You got your twenty bucks, now beat it."

"Leggo!" Lester gasped.

Gerald looked at me and said, "O.K., Harry? Can I let him go?"

I grinned at him and shrugged. "You think he's going to be a good boy, Gerald?"

"Well, are you Lester?" Gerald said, giving the biker's neck a hard jerk.

Lester nodded spasmodically. "Leggo!"

Gerald let him go and, in one motion, jerked open the side door and pulled the biker out onto the sidewalk. Lester sat on the pavement for a second and rubbed his sore neck.

"That wasn't a Christian thing to do, Gerald," he said with high dudgeon.

Gerald gave him a hard kick in the butt, and Lester scampered back across Edwards to the Tic-Toc parking lot.

"That really wasn't very Christian, Gerald," I said to him as he sat down beside me on the front seat.

"Maybe not," he said with a grin. "But it shore felt good to mix it up again." He looked at me hopefully. "Did I do all right?"

"You did just fine," I told him.

I dropped Gerald Arnold back off at his apartment on Ogden and told him if he ever got tired of the night shift at Ford I might be able to find a use for him.

"No shit?" he said proudly.

"You'd have to cut your hair a bit, though."

That dampened his enthusiasm. "Well, I'll think it over, Harry," he said. "And I'll see what Brother Stearns has to say."

He wasn't very bright, Gerald. But he was strong and

quick and he had the kind of inborn loyalty that no amount of money can buy. In spite of his hair and his teeth and his jittery manner, Gerald had a man's heart. And there are times in my work when nothing else will do.

He walked off to Clancy & Sons apartment house and I backed onto Ogden, drove up to Madison, and then headed north to Withrow and to Assistant Principal Rogers, who just might be able to tell me what I wanted to know about Hack and his loyal brother.

It was about noon when I pulled into the Withrow lot and the place was crowded with kids going to or coming back from lunch. From what I could see through the car window, times hadn't changed very much at Withrow High. I recognized the same faces I'd known when I was a high school kid. Greasers in leather jackets, sneaking a smoke on the hood of a Chevy. Girls with their hair tied back in ribbons, hugging their notebooks to their breasts and swaying slightly at the hips as if they were dancing in a dream. Pretty girls dressed in Sasson jeans and Vanderbilt tops, long-legging it past the others as if they were just visiting for the day. Jocks who were all neck and shoulders. The studious ones with calculators on their belts and pencils growing from their shirt pockets like untrimmed hedges. I passed through the crowd and up the front steps into that long, U-shaped, red brick building, down concrete corridors lined with gray metal lockers, past wooden doors that opened on rooms full of desks and blackboards and the sunlight that spilled through the tall schoolhouse windows, to the assistant principal's office—a small, glassed-in complex furnished with two secretary's desks and a switchboard set behind a long formica counter. The sign on the door at the south side of the room said "Assistant Principal."

"I'm looking for Mr. Rogers," I said to the girl sitting behind the counter—a schoolgirl in a white blouse and a tartan-plaid skirt. "My name is Stoner. Tell him I want to speak to him about Haskell Lord."

"I'll see if he's in," she said and pressed a buzzer on the intercom.

Rogers answered in a deep businessman's voice. When he heard the name Haskell Lord, he said he'd be right out and, a moment later, he came through the door. He was a tall, dour-looking man with sparse brown hair and the kind of rubbery-featured face that looks as if someone has hooked their thumbs in the corners of the mouth then pulled downward, stretching it into a melancholy mask. It was a Walter Matthau face. And it, too, was familiar from my own distant youth. He was wearing a business suit, flecked with dandruff on the shoulders, and his arms were cocked awkwardly in front of him, as if he were holding a box of dynamite in his hands.

"Mr. Stoner?" he said.

I told him I was Stoner. He shook my hand and ushered me into his office.

"You know a Ms. Davis was here yesterday asking me about Haskell," he said as he sat down behind his school house desk. He placed the box of dynamite on the desktop in front of him, stared at it for a minute, and then very slowly dropped his hands to either side. He took a deep breath and sat back in his chair. Poor Rogers was literally carrying his charge around with him, and given the volatile nature of our high schools, it must have been a pretty dangerous charge. It certainly looked dangerous to Rogers, who kept eyeing it as we talked, as if he were half afraid it would go off if his back were turned. "As I told her yesterday, I've seen Haskell on several occasions since he graduated. Most recently a few months ago up on the track. He looked awful. Haggard, physically debilitated. I could hardly believe he was the same boy who graduated eight years ago." He rubbed his eyes wearily and said, "I doubt if I would have recognized him at all if I hadn't seen his brother with him."

Well, Harry, I said to myself, there's a bit of confirmation. "Did Jake always accompany his brother?" I asked him.

"I couldn't say. I don't remember seeing the two of them apart. But then that's not uncommon with teenage brothers. You'd be better off talking to Miss Gibson, our counselor, if you're interested in how the two of them related to each other and to their teachers and classmates. She has an office above mine on the second floor."

"Did you know that Hack was selling speed outside the school?"

Rogers didn't even raise an eyebrow. "No, I did not. But it doesn't surprise me. You know those people who complain about the quality of the city school system ought to take the time to come here and look around. It's not what the kids take away from here that's so disheartening. It's what they bring with them in the way of attitudes and values. That's what's really shocking, Mr. Stoner. No, it doesn't surprise me that some of my students should be buying speed outside the school. Or smoking pot. Or shooting heroin. I've given up being surprised. And then Haskell was always a hard case. Always moody and borderline violent. Quite talented and intelligent, nevertheless."

"You don't know of any particular students who might have done business with him, do you? Or who might know where he is now?"

Rogers reached into his desk and pulled out a roster

sheet. He tossed it over to me. "Pick a name, Mr. Stoner."

I glanced at the sheet. There must have been a hundred students listed on it.

"You see that's what an assistant principal does," Rogers said with a sigh. "I am responsible for what is laughingly called discipline. That list that you're holding contains the names of the boys and girls who've been in detention this week alone."

"Surely there are some students who have serious problems with drugs?" I said.

"Whole classrooms full. We have children—and I mean twelve and thirteen years old—nodding off their chairs every day. I could give you a list of particular troublemakers. But it would be a long list. And the chances of any of them talking honestly with you would be very small. You see," Rogers said with a tight-lipped grin, "they don't trust us."

Rogers gripped his box of dynamite again and got up from his chair. "I'll take you up to Miss Gibson's office, if you wish. Sometimes she can be a little hard to talk to."

I gave him a quizzical look and he shrugged.

"She doesn't have an easy job," he said.

21

ANDREA GIBSON had a sign on her desk that read "Have a good day!" She had a "have a good day" clock on the wall and a "have a good day" button on her blouse. The room was filled with so many smiling, insipid faces that her own face came as something of a shock. If you squeezed that jolly "good day" face hard enough to make the eyes pop wide open and the small mouth pucker into a fishy "O," if you capped it with a curly wig the color of scrap metal and then perched it on a plain white blouse with lapels the size of lobster bibs, you might have come up with an Andrea Gibson. Or with a Marion Lorne. The two were one, as far as I could see. Right down to the dotty befuddled look on their faces and the husky hesitant voice. Rogers spent a moment introducing us, although I wasn't quite sure whether Miss Gibson was convinced. In fact the first thing she asked me when Rogers left the room was: "Are you really a detective?"

When I said yes, she looked confused and said, "How very odd."

"It has that effect on most people."

"It does?" she said and then she laughed, or tittered, with the tuneless precision of an alarm clock. "I see. You were making a joke. I must be slow today. Friday's are a slow day for me."

I had the feeling that most days were slow days for Andrea Gibson, who had all the makings of an incompetent. Her type was familiar enough. A superannuated librarian or grammar teacher who'd lost her nerve, she'd been shuffled upstairs to serve out her last years before retirement. And beyond prescribing an occasional aspirin or administering a dose of MMPT, her sole advice to the dozens of students who passed daily through that neat little office was to "have a good day." She did not inspire me with confidence. But as it turned out, I was not being at all fair to Miss Andrea Gibson.

"You came to talk about Haskell Lord?" she said in that bemused voice.

I said I had.

And she said, "That doesn't surprise me. He had a very unfortunate childhood."

I told her that I knew about as much as I needed to know about Hack's background and that I was more concerned with how he related to his brother.

"Oh, but the two are connected," she said with a round, unappeasable smile.

I could see that she was going to give me her view of the matter whether I wanted her to or not, so I put a polite look on my face and asked her to explain again how Hack's selfish, implacable mother and his polite, idealistic brother had turned a troubled boy into a killer. And she did. But with an interesting twist.

"Do you know what a scapegoat is, Mr. Stoner?" she said with innocent pedantry. "Joseph Addison wrote an interesting essay about it three hundred years ago. Of course, we figure that we know a great deal more about the mind now than Addison did at the beginning of the eighteenth century. And in some ways we do. When I took my degree in psychology, psychoanalysis was all the rage. Since then there's been a revolution in psychotherapy—a pharmacological revolution. And what we were taught to think of as quirks of the libido are being proved to be prodigies of chemistry. Sometimes I think that science isn't getting more precise, just smaller. More minute. If you can see the difference." She looked up suddenly and said, "Do you think I'm odd?"

I blushed and said, "A little."

"Well, I am," she said with that tuneless laugh. "My students know it. You can't fool them. They're attuned to deceptions. They have to be to deal with those creatures we call parents. I was born three hundred years behind the times, because, you see, I think Addison and the moral philosophers were right. There are chemistries and chemistries. And where the heart is concerned, it's human chemistry that counts. Don't you agree?"

"I think I do," I said.

"A good answer," she said. "Now, lest you think I'm a total fool, allow me to explain what I meant. In families like Haskell Lord's—indeed, in many so-called 'normal' fami-

196

lies, as well—relationships have become so weighted down with guilts and anxieties that the 'healthy' expression of emotions—a phrase that, I confess, I've never entirely understood—is grossly inhibited. When a parent dies or goes to prison or loses his job or divorces, the whole family suffers the trauma. Everyone shares in the blame. Ideally, that guilt would be expiated through open discussion, through work and recreation and, above all, through love. The great panacea. Truly the only commonplace that I never deplore. But when love itself becomes sick, as it has in the Lord family, then that vital sympathy is cut off. Since the trauma will not go away on its own, the family has to find another way to exorcise its individual and collective guilts. Which brings us back to Mr. Addison and the theory of scapegoats. You're familiar, of course, with the notion of a 'black sheep'?"

I told her that I'd heard the phrase once or twice, and she smiled.

"Some families create them," she said, "the way other families celebrate achievements. A scapegoat or a black sheep isn't merely a person, it's a piece of machinery, a psychical pump through which the whole family, even the scapegoat himself, channels its guilts and aggressions—all of those feelings that, through lack of love, they can't safely express to each other or to themselves. Black sheep are very necessary things. Why in some families, they are all that hold a group of virtual strangers together. Indeed, there are many instances of families collapsing—nervous breakdowns, divorces, sudden acts of violence—after a so-called black sheep mends his or her way and reforms."

"And you're saying that the Lord family is an example of your scapegoat theory?" I said.

"But, of course. A perfect example. I don't know why the

mother decided to make Haskell the black sheep, instead of Jacob. Haskell was the eldest and the more overtly violent of the two. And potentially the most dangerous. But both brothers have severe personality disorders. And while I've never interviewed her, I'd be willing to bet that the mother is the most disturbed of the three."

"You know what Hack has done?" I said to her.

She nodded. "I've done a great deal of thinking about the Lord family since yesterday. Understand, I'm not trying to excuse Haskell. All of my tests showed marked sociopathic tendencies in the boy. What used to be called misanthropy. Coupled with homicidal urges. He is certainly a very disturbed and very dangerous young man. All I'm really saying is what is obvious to anyone—nobody goes crazy all by himself. From what I've observed, the whole family is a little mad."

I'd been dead wrong about Andrea Gibson. She was anything but the passed-over incompetent that I thought she was, although she clearly wanted to encourage an eccentric impression, perhaps because it made it easier to communicate with those creatures known as children. And with glib detectives, too. I asked her with genuine interest whether she thought Jake was capable of shielding his brother in spite of what Hack had done, whether that would fit her "black sheep" theory. And she pursed her round lips and thought it out.

"It's hard to say," she said after a moment. "Jacob's relationship with his brother is intriguing—I mean, of course, from a professional point of view. From all appearances, the two of them were inseparable friends. And yet I know from talking to Haskell that he resented his brother's constant attention. Nor was it ever clear to me whether Jacob's friendship was entirely unambivalent. He certainly had a passionate attachment to his brother. But I think he was more than a little angry at Haskell, too, for allowing himself to be so thoroughly victimized by their mother. I sense a cold rage beneath that fulsome politeness of his. And to answer your question, yes, I think it's possible that Jacob would protect his older brother."

"Even though Haskell has murdered two women?"

"Perhaps because of that, Mr. Stoner," she said without blinking an eye. "Haskell was the black sheep, remember? And Jacob has had a great deal of practice blaming and excusing his brother for all that's gone wrong in both of their lives. He may not be able to function without that crutch."

"I hope you're right," I said. "Because right now Jacob is all I've got to go on."

"In a way," she said. "I hope I'm not."

"Why?"

"Because I'd like to see one of those benighted souls come out of this whole," Andrea Gibson said. "You might do me a favor, Mr. Stoner."

"I'll try."

"If you do find Haskell, as you must, try to keep Jacob away from the . . . what should I call it?" she said heavily. "Don't let him see his brother die, Mr. Stoner. That's what I mean."

I told her again that I'd try.

22

LIKE BENSON Howell, Andrea Gibson had left me with a good deal to think about—none of it pleasant. It was time, I decided, for a meeting of the minds. When I got back to the library at two, I plucked Kate Davis off her second-floor perch and led her down to Ringold's office, where she and I had a chat. Ringold himself had been called downtown to talk with what Miss Moselle called the "big boys," so we had his spare little office to ourselves. Or, at least, I thought we had. There really wasn't any way to tell what kind of bugs or peepholes the little old ladies might have planted in the room. Anyway, we spoke as if we were speaking for an audience. And what we talked about was how to deal with Jacob Lord.

"I don't think I believe it, Harry," Kate said when I'd finished telling her what Miss Gibson had told me. "He seems so forthright to me. Defensive, of course. Who wouldn't be under the same circumstances. But not at all the kind of person who would deliberately mislead us."

I fiddled with one of Ringold's number two pencils. It looked as if he'd been gnawing on it with chagrin. There were toothmarks on the eraser. "I agree that he doesn't seem to be the type. But he hasn't been entirely forthright, as you put it, with us. He lied about not having seen Hack in years. He lied about what Hack was doing up at Withrow. He didn't tell me that Hack was a speed freak when he sent me off on that pleasant little jaunt to Norris Reaves's barn. Which almost got me killed, if you remember."

"But that doesn't mean he's hiding Hack somewhere."

"I'm not saying that he is. Only that he might know where Hack is holed-up." I dropped the pencil in the tray and said, "Kate, he's been following his brother around most of his life—for whatever the reasons. It doesn't seem probable that he'd stop now. And the truth is, we don't have anything else to go on."

Kate stared glumly at the desk. "This is my fault, damn it, for not digging up a clue to his next victim."

I laughed at her. Which was a mistake.

Her face turned an angry shade of red and for a moment I thought she was going to sock me. "You really don't think I can cut the mustard, do you, Harry," she said indignantly.

"If you want to have a fight, Kate, go ahead. But you're fighting with yourself."

"No, damn it, I'm fighting with you. You're a chauvinist.

Not an outrageous chauvinist—you've got too good a heart for that. But a chauvinist, nevertheless. And I'm getting tired of being put on the back burner everytime you think it's for the best. I don't want somebody deciding what's good for me. I want to make my own decisions and I don't want to be laughed at for doing it."

There was no sense in explaining to her that I wasn't laughing at her powers of will or of mind. And any attempt to justify myself by pointing out that I knew more about the detective business than she did would have been scorned as a rationalization. Besides, that wasn't the reason I was being protective. There's a helluva fine line between chauvinism and what she had called "good-heartedness," although, I suppose, it's a line that's always going to have to be redrawn between two strong-willed adults who happen to be in love.

So I did the safe thing and the sane one. I apologized. She looked abashed, as if that was the last thing on earth she'd expected me to say, and sat back sullenly on her chair.

"Apology accepted," she said after a time. "Anyway it was a stupid thing for me to say. Dropping me off at the library a couple of hours ago didn't do much for my ego, you know."

I knew. And I also knew that we'd just missed having an explosive argument that could have sent us both storming off in a rage. I was a little proud of us.

"Now what are we going to do about Jacob?" I asked her.

"I guess we could follow him," she said.

"Yeah, but he knows who we are. And he also knows that the police are watching his house. If he is shielding his brother, he's going to be very careful about any contact with Hack. Besides, following him could be a very long process. And there's no need to point out how important it is to get our hands on Haskell before he kills again."

"We could get a search warrant from your friend George DeVries. Maybe there's something in the house or in Hack's room that could lead us to him."

"It's a good thought," I said. "Only the cops already paid the Lord house a visit yesterday and didn't turn up a thing. What we have to do is give Jake an urgent reason to get in touch with Hack. An unimpeachable reason. Something that will send him straight to his brother."

"If he really does know where he's hiding," Kate said without much conviction. "And besides, if he's gone to so much trouble to protect Haskell, what would make him bolt and run?"

It was a damn good question.

Al Foster had a few laconic suggestions to make when we gathered in his tiny office at three-thirty that afternoon. And George DeVries, who'd finally managed to convince Walker Parsons that it would be a good idea to cash in on Haskell before the end of the month, had a few brutal ideas of his own. But it wasn't until half-past four, when Cal Levy came down from Harrison to join our strategy session, that we got our first real break.

We'd been discussing the merits of tailing Jake with plainclothesmen, and tempers were getting hot. The office was so small that we were almost sitting on top of each other. And it had begun to rain around four, so it was humid as well as cramped in the tiny room. Then George had gotten huffy when Kate had violently disagreed with his plan to drag Jake into Station X and beat the truth out of him. And all hell broke loose. It was a typical DeVries suggestion, vicious and expedient. But Kate didn't know much about George or about police procedures. And the fact that he'd been calling her "little lady" since the moment we'd stepped through the door hadn't helped either.

"We're not even sure that he knows where Hack is!" she finally exploded. "This isn't a police state where you can just pull anybody you want in off the street and torture them into telling you what want to hear."

Al flashed me his version of a smile and I stared at the floor. What Kate had objected to was standard police practice. Dragging suspects in off the street and subjecting them to forty or fifty hours of grilling under hot lights was all in a day's work.

"Who the hell is this woman anyway?" DeVries thundered. "Aren't you the little lady who was going to karate the Ripper into submission?"

Kate's face turned red and she clenched her fists.

"Take it easy," I said quickly. "Everybody."

"What's she doing here anyway?" DeVries said. "She doesn't need to be in on this case anymore."

"She's here, George," I said, "because she deserves to be. If it weren't for her, we wouldn't know that the Ripper killed Twyla. Without Kate, we wouldn't have a case at all."

He mumbled something under his breath about women and the best place for them. And Kate mumbled something back about what he could do with himself when he found the time. Then both of them curled up in their chairs and stared daggers at each other while Al and I continued to talk.

"We didn't really search the house, Harry," he said, plucking a fresh Tareyton from his coat. "Just the once over and a talk with the mother and with Jake. It might not be a bad idea to take another look, if we can get the kid out of the house for a time so he doesn't doctor things up or get in the way."

"That might not be so easy," I said. "He seems to hang around the house a lot. Does anybody have an idea of what he does for a living?"

Al pulled a notepad from his desk drawer. "He was a student at D.A.A. for awhile. Or so his mother says. Right now he's 'looking for suitable employment.'"

"D.A.A.?" DeVries said suddenly. "That's the University art school, isn't it?"

"Yeah," I said.

"Well that's probably how Hack first spotted Twyla," he said. "A lot of those art students hang around together. And since he and Jake were such close buddies, he might have spotted her at a meeting or a get-together that they had."

It was a reasonable guess. Hack could have begun following her after that. Watched her in the library. Cut up the books. And then . . .

"We've got to get Jake out of that house," I said. "We've got to get him to lead us to Hack. Now how the hell are we going to do that?"

Nobody had a decent suggestion until Cal Levy walked into the room in his calf-skin boots and his Stetson, with his silver-plated .45 on his hip.

"Sorry I'm late," he said, swiping the hat off his head and shaking rainwater off the brim. "It's plumb nasty out there. And then I had a D&D to look after." He glanced at the room. "Mighty crowded in here, ain't it?"

"That isn't the half of it," DeVries said.

Al and I filled him in on the situation. He listened attentively, as if he expected to be quizzed on the details when we were done. Then he hooked his thumbs in his belt and said, "I think I might be able to help."

"Go on," Al said.

"Well, it's like this. We've been following up on this drug thing that Harry unearthed out in Dent. See, it struck me as kind of strange that Norris Reaves was so damn certain that Haskell'd spill the beans if we got our hands on him. Made me think he might know a good deal more about Hack than he was saying. Old Norris ain't too bright. But you'd be surprised how smart a man can get when his life's at stake. Hearing about what happened to Effie didn't shake him up none. Said he'd expected it, ever since she began hanging around with Hack. He knew that Lord was going to be the death of her, one way or another. But she just wouldn't listen to reason. What finally got him talking was the prospect of fifteen years to life for attempted murder and drug trafficking. Now that really touched him where he lived. I had a long chat with him this morning and when I let it be known that I might do some dickering—maybe knock the attempted murder charge down to assault, if he told me what he knew about Hack—he got real cooperative. Hack was in a bad way last time Norris seen him. Strung out and mean and 'bout half-starved, I guess, from the speed. He didn't know for sure where Hack had gone after Effie give him the boot. But he said there was an old farmhouse out in Milford that Hack used to talk about when he was stoned. It was a place him and his brother used to go to when they wanted to get away from their mother. That is, before Hack met Effie. Norris thinks Hack might be hiding out there."

"Where in Milford?" I said.

Cal Levy shook his head. "Don't know. And I'll tell you

the truth, I ain't even sure Milford is right. Prospect of a jail cell can make an unimaginative man downright fanciful."

"Well, it's something," Al Foster said. "Now what are we going to do with it?"

"Feed it to Jake," I said. "And see what happens."

"And what makes you think anything *will* happen?" Kate said.

"A little old lady named Andrea Gibson," I said. "And a theory she has about black sheep."

At six that night we assembled at the library—Al Foster, Cal Levy, George DeVries, a couple of plainclothesmen, and Kate and I—synchronized our watches, just like in the war movies, and set Plan Final Notice (Miss Moselle's somewhat morbid suggestion) to work. At six-forty, the two plainclothesmen were scheduled to walk through the rain up to the Lord's front door. The rest of us would be scattered at various spots up and down Stettinius. The plainclothesmen were to tell Jake that they'd had a tip that his brother was hiding out in Milford. He hadn't been pinned down, yet. But there was going to be a house-to-house search of the whole area in the morning. Jake was to stay by the phone in case Hack called. All calls would be monitored.

The plainclothesmen would drive off, and if Miss Gibson were right and Jake really did feel that mixture of devotion, anger, and guilt that bonded him to his brother, and if he did know where he was, and if there was a childhood hideaway in Milford, then he'd lead us to him. And once he'd delivered his warning—judging by what Lester the speed freak had told me, the same warning he must have been giving Hack all his life, that admonition that was his peculiar form of brotherly love—we'd close in on Haskell Lord.

207

There were an awful lot of "ifs" in that formula. An awful lot that could go wrong, as Miss Moselle, who'd been lending an ear, quickly pointed out. Even to me it sounded vaguely ridiculous—the plotting of a television melodrama. Things just didn't work that neatly in the real world, even if that neatness was a true reflection of the symmetry of Lord family life, of what Miss Moselle might term the Capricorn-like fit of Jake and Haskell's psyches.

"I may be wrong," Jessie said, "but it seems to me that Jacob could simply drive to a pay phone and ring his brother up, without even taking you any closer to his hiding place than that. Of course there may not be a phone in this farmhouse. Still, it's something to consider."

Al and George looked at me and I shook my head. I was beginning to feel a little sympathy for Ringold.

"And there's no guarantee," Kate added, "that Norris Reaves *was* telling the truth. Hack doesn't have to be in Milford. He could be anywhere."

"Just what the hell do you ladies suggest we do?" George DeVries said.

We all looked at Miss Moselle, who pinked a little, cleared her throat, and said, "If I'm not being too bold, would it not be judicious to—what is the word—divide your forces? Perhaps Mrs. Lord knows something of this boyhood hideaway. I mean, of course, if it does exist. And then there's always the possibility that you might find something of value—a clue—in the boy's room. Haskell is an artist, after all. Perhaps he drew a sketch of his hiding place?"

"Waste of time," DeVries said.

But I wasn't so sure. Hack had left those drawings in Effie's trailer as a clue. Art or its destruction seem to run through the case like a theme. Cal Levy agreed with me.

"Sounds right smart," he said.

208

So after a bit of debate, we modified the plan to the degree that Kate would stay behind at the Lord home while the rest of us followed Jake. I was a little surprised at how quickly Kate acquiesced, seeing that DeVries, in particular, had made it clear that she'd be better off out of the way. But when I asked her, as we walked out to the parking lot, why she'd changed her mind about helping to catch the Ripper, she said, "I haven't. But if catching the Ripper means watching a man like DeVries shoot him down in cold blood, I'm willing to forgo the pleasure."

"That's not going to happen," I said. "Not unless Hack makes it happen."

She shook her head and said, "I wouldn't bet on it. Besides I think I have a better chance of locating our Ripper at the Lord house than you do off in Milford."

"Maybe," I said. "But if you do come up with something, Kate, for chrissake, don't go after him on your own."

"I may be headstrong, Harry," she said with a wink, "but I'm not an idiot."

23

AT SIX-THIRTY, Kate and I drove through the rain to Stettinius and parked about three doors down from the Lord house. At six-forty on the nose, the plainclothesmen pulled up in a blue-and-white city car. We watched them through the rain-spattered windshield as they walked briskly up to the Lord front door—two husky men in green raincoats and khaki hats, with tough, efficient looks on their faces.

"Now keep your fingers crossed," I said to Kate.

The door opened and Jake stepped out onto the stoop. He smiled his subdued, choirboy's smile and the two men began their spiel. Jake stopped them once, with an up-turned palm, then pointed with his arm to the street, as if he were trying to get his geography straight. One of the agents nodded and said a few more words.

"That's it," I said. "They've given him the bait."

The two cops turned on their heels and walked back down to their car. Jake kept an eye on them as they drove off, then looked back through the door with something like resignation—as if he'd caught sight of his mother standing at the foot of the stairs. He walked slowly into the house, closing the door behind him.

"Now what?" Kate whispered with excitement.

And I realized, suddenly, that I was excited. too. After a week of groping about, after Twyla and Effie and Norris and that barn, I'd have to have been a lot less sanguine than I was not to have gotten excited.

"Now we sit back," I said. "And hope that Jake swallows the bait."

By ten o'clock most of our excitement had drained away. No one had stirred inside the Lord house. No one had even come to the window. We'd shifted around on the car seat a couple dozen times. Played a few games of twenty questions. (Mona Lisa, turnstile, Jake Lord.) Necked a little. And finally understood that Final Notice wasn't going to work.

It should have worked. By all psychological rights, Jake Lord should have come surging out the door—to reproach and clean up after his prodigal brother. Only Jake didn't come out. Which meant one of two things—either he knew that his brother wasn't in Milford or, after two murders and a police investigation, he'd finally given up on Haskell and decided to face the world without the help of a scapegoat he could blame for all of his problems.

Kate was being polite. But I could tell from her Cheshire grin that she was a little satisfied that her theory was being proved right—that Jake was just a nice young man with a sex murderer for a brother.

"We can still search the house," she said with a peak of pleasure in her voice.

"He's going to come out," I said. "Just give him time."

"Maybe he has an invisible car?"

"Shut up, Kate," I said.

She sat back on the car seat and smiled.

"You've just never been on a stake-out before," I said haughtily. "Sometimes it takes days before you get a response."

"Years," Kate Davis said.

"Maybe if we gave him another dose of the cops?"

"Told him the bloodhounds were being trucked out to Milford at twelve?"

"I'm thinking of a thing, Kate," I said. "And I don't think you'd want to know what it is."

"Everybody makes mistakes," she said.

And I said, "Shit."

Two more hours went by. In the rain and the cold. My good spirits were wearing thin. And Kate's were just about worn out.

"It's not working, Harry," she said. "And my ass is turning blue."

"I could warm it up for you."

She giggled and said, "Maybe later."

And at that moment, after almost six hours of waiting, I heard a car start up behind the Lord house.

"He's probably going out for a doughnut," Kate said. But her voice was stern and when I looked at her face, there was no playfulness left in it.

"I'll be O.K.," I said.

I bent down and kissed her lips. She wrapped her arms around my neck and whispered, "Please be careful, darling. And don't do anything heroic."

"And you, too."

We kissed again—for a long moment—then I hopped out of the Pinto and dashed across Stettinius to Al Foster's Chevy. DeVries and Cal Levy were sitting in the back seat.

"All right, boys," Foster said. "Let's go."

For above ten minutes, none of us was sure exactly where Jacob Lord was leading us. He wandered up and down the suburban streets of Hyde Park as if he weren't quite sure himself about where he was going. When he turned on Erie, I thought we'd lost him.

"He's going home," I said to Foster. "Goddamn it! He's going home."

I held my breath as he coasted toward Stettinius. Al had to lay back a good half-mile because of the light traffic, so all I could see were the red pinpoints of his taillights and a trickle of smoke coming from the exhaust pipe.

Jake got to Stettinius, stopped momentarily at a stop sign on the corner, then continued down Erie. We all let out a whoop, because he was headed east now, toward the interstate that led to Milford. He turned north on Ridge and picked up the expressway in Norwood. We swooped down the ramp after him, through the concrete interstices of the overpass, and out along 71 where it winds through the Montgomery hillsides. The roadway was dark and misty where it cut through the hills, the only light coming from the ranch houses set back on the wooded slopes and from the red taillights of the cars in front of us. No one in the car had said a thing for over five minutes, because it had become apparent that Jacob *was* going to take us where we

213

wanted to go, that after six hours of deliberation he was finally going to lead us to the sleepy hamlet of Milford on the eastern edge of the county and to a showdown with his brother, Hack. The only thing that bothered me was why it had taken him six hours to make up his mind. I patted my coat pocket nervously. It was there, all right, the big Colt Commander with its nine-shot clip. I patted it again, sat back in the car seat and waited.

By the time we got to the 275 interchange, we'd all begun to get a little nervous. You could smell the fear in the hot smokey air of the car. Over the cigarette smells and the musty, electric smell of the heater, the keen, wilting smell of fear.

"I guess we'd better plan things out," Foster said abruptly.

"What's to plan?" George said. "We take him as soon as the kid goes inside the house."

I thought of Andrea Gibson and said, "What happens to Jake? What if his brother decides to make a fight of it?"

"There are four of us," DeVries said.

"That's not what I meant. The way Jake feels about Haskell, he might do something foolish. And I don't want to see him get hurt."

"He's harboring a felon, for chrissake!" DeVries said.

"He's protecting his brother, George. And that's not a shooting offense. I think we should wait until the kid comes back out the door before we make our move."

"What if Hack comes out with him?" Levy said.

"Then one of us knocks Jake down and out of the way, and the other three tackle Hack."

"It's O.K. by me," Cal Levy said.

214

Foster didn't say anything and DeVries clucked his tongue.

"That boy in there is a certified lunatic," George said. "He could be armed to the teeth. And all you can think about is hearts and flowers. I'll tell you this, if Hack or his brother so much as flashes a piece of iron, I'm taking both their heads off with a shotgun. And I'll cry about it later."

We continued on I-71 to 275 east, and then Jake veered off at the Batavia exit. He turned north on 27 and before we knew it, we were in flat, fenced-in farm country—acres and acres of rain-swept fields and white slat farmhouses. Al had to lay back a good distance because we were the only traffic on the road. I was studying the tiny pinpricks of Jake's taillights when they disappeared.

"What the hell happened!" DeVries said.

Foster said, "He turned off."

Al flipped off his headlights and we coasted to a stop about a hundred yards south of where Jake had turned off in the Buick.

"Can you see a house?" DeVries said.

I stared through the side window. All I could make out through the curtain of tree branches was a glimmer of white board, like a tatter of cloth caught on a strand of fencing. There were no lights at all along the road or out in the muddy fields. And no sounds but the plinking of the rain on the car roof and the swishing of the willow branches in the wind.

"All right," Foster said. "Here's what we're going to do. Cal, you and George take the east side of the house. Harry and I will take the west. If the kid comes out without his brother—fine. Let him pass. If Hack comes out the door after him, we wait until they're in the clear and rush them. That is, unless either one of them is carrying a weapon in his hand. Who's the best shot here?"

Cal Levy said, "I ain't bad with a rifle."

"Right," Foster said. "There's a 30-06 in the trunk of the car along with a pump shotgun. Cal, you take the rifle and George will take the scatter gun. If Hack comes out of that house carrying a gun, Cal, I want you to drop him where he stands. If he hasn't got a weapon, we'll rush him. And, George, don't get trigger happy or you may end up shooting one of us." Foster picked up the transceiver and called in to Station X. He gave them our location and requested a S.W.A.T. team and a negotiator, in case Haskell decided that he wasn't coming out on his own. "They won't make it out here for at least three quarters of an hour, so until then it's up to us." He cracked open the side door and said, "Let's go."

We piled out of the car, got the weapons and a bullhorn from the trunk, then filed up the road. A line of maples and willows strung along the roadside shielded us from the house. Then we got lucky and the rain died down to a drizzle, making it a helluva lot easier to see.

When we got to the turn-off, I ran ahead to size things up.

The Buick was parked on a gravel lane that lead up to a dilapidated two-story farm house, set in a stand of pine trees. There were no phone or power lines leading to the house. Which was why Jake hadn't made a call. Pines lined either side of the gravel lane—good cover for us. But there were trees behind the house, too. Which meant that one of us was going to have to keep his eye on the rear door. Al Foster came up behind me as I was thinking things out.

216

"Cal and George are on the other side of the road," he whispered.

"Somebody's going to have to take the back door," I whispered in return.

He nodded. "Let's try to work our way up to the porch."

We sidled through the pine trees, moving from trunk to trunk. Al covering me as I moved ahead and then me covering him. The damn pines were full of rainwater. With the wind blowing, I was soaked to the skin by the time we got to the house, and Al's rubbery face looked like a lump of clay that had been left out in a storm.

"Helluva way to make a living," he whispered acidly.

We huddled behind the trunk of a pine and stared at the porch. We were only twenty feet away from it, now. Close enough to get a clear view of anyone coming out the front door. The Buick was parked about forty feet behind us, in the center of the gravel lane. If Jake and Haskell didn't spot us, we could take them from behind as they walked out to the car. I pulled the Colt from my pocket and flipped off the safety.

There wasn't a sound for better than ten minutes. Then the front door opened and Jake stepped out onto the porch. He was alone and he was carrying something in his hand. I couldn't make out what it was until he was halfway down the steps. It looked like a paper shopping bag, and whatever he was carrying in it was heavy enough to make him lean slightly to his right.

Now what the hell's going on? I said to myself. Maybe it was food he'd brought for Haskell. But there was something else peculiar about the way he looked. I couldn't put my finger on it until he was in the Buick and driving back up the lane. He hadn't looked excited or worried—the way he should have looked under the circumstances. What I could see of his face was mournful and subdued, as if he were coming out of a church rather than out of a killer's lair.

"He must still be in there," Foster said to me, as we watched Jake's taillights disappear down the lane. "We're going to have to pry him loose."

"Swell," I said.

Al raised the bullhorn to his mouth and flipped on the battery. The horn made a high-pitched whine, like the ear-splitting peak of an improperly balanced microphone. It made me jump. It had probably made Haskell Lord jump, too. Wired on speed. Half-starved and crazy. It had probably made him jump right out of his skin. I studied the upstairs windows. But nobody looked out. There wasn't a sound from the house at all. Not even the creak of a floor-board.

"Haskell Lord!" Al said into the bullhorn and the whole yard echoed his voice. "This is the police! We have the house surrounded. Come out with your hands raised."

Al put the horn down and winked at me. "Never got a chance to say that before in my life."

There wasn't a sound from that broken-down house.

"Something isn't right," I said to Al.

He raised the horn again and shouted, "Haskell! We know you're in there. Don't make us come in after you."

Someone came rushing across the yard.

"Easy, Harry," Al said. "I think it's DeVries."

George ducked behind the pine tree where we were standing and said, "You know what? I don't think he's in there."

"The hell," Foster said.

"No. I'm serious," DeVries said. "I took a look through

218

the back window and didn't see a thing. Couldn't hear a thing either. It's all torn-up in there. Just a shell, really. And I'm telling you nobody could hold his breath in that place or just stand in one spot without making a little noise."

"Well if he isn't in there," Foster said. "Why the hell did Jake lead us all the way out here in the middle of the night?"

Nobody said a thing for a moment.

"Maybe we'd better take a look inside," I told them.

24

THE TAIL had been my idea, so I was the first one through the door. It wasn't locked, but George blew it off its hinges with the shotgun anyway. Kate had been right about that much—he was intent on shooting something that night. When the cordite smoke had cleared, I scampered through the hole into a pitch-black room, full of plaster chips and broken glass that crunched like rock salt underfoot. If Hack were in the house, he sure as hell knew we were coming. Foster followed me in—his service pistol in one hand and a heavy-duty flashlight he'd dug out of the trunk in the other. The flashlight beam danced about the room, touching on some exposed timber in the wall and a crack in the dusty wood floor and one rusted beer can that was sitting in a corner. The room stank of mildew and of woodrot and of something else, something sweeter and more frightening.

Cal Levy said it for all of us when he walked through the doorway. "Somethin's died in here."

"An animal, maybe," DeVries said.

"I don't think so. It's too strong a stink."

We looked at each other for a second, and I thought of that remote and mournful look on Jake Lord's face.

"I've got a real bad feeling about this house," I said. To no one in particular. To myself, I think.

"Let's take a look around," Al said nervously. "George, you and Cal take the ground floor. We'll look upstairs."

The staircase was located in a hall that connected the front room with what looked like an old kitchen or what was left of a kitchen—a rusted wash basin dangling from the wall and an old refrigerator lying on its side in the dirt with the smug, encroaching look of a coffin. The staircase itself was in pretty good shape, except for a few boards at the bottom that had been bitten in two by time and weather. When Al passed the flashlight beam up to the top landing, I saw footprints in the dust. Two or three sets of a man's shoe-print. Someone had been walking up and down the stairs recently. Maybe on behalf of someone else on the second floor. I nudged Al with my elbow and he said, "Yeah, I see them."

I started up the staircase, the pistol in my right hand.

"Keep that damn beam in front of me, Al," I said over my shoulder. "I don't want to run into any surprises."

Up we went, the flashlight leaping from stair to stair in front of us. Then we reached the landing and the death smell became so strong that I almost gagged.

"It's up here, all right," I said to Al and he nodded grimly.

The staircase opened on a hallway that ran the length of the top floor. Three rooms—two on the east side of the hall, one on the west—were scattered along the corridor. Each one was closed off by a painted wooden door.

"Take your pick, Harry," Al said drily.

I sniffed the air and said, "Let's start at the back. I think that's where the smell is strongest."

We walked down the hallway to the rear room.

"You ready?" I said.

Al grunted.

I put my hand to the door knob and pushed the door open. Al flashed the beam into the room.

His eyes were the first thing we saw, glimmering in the light the way a rat's eye glimmers in the beam of a headlight. Only they didn't wink shut, as they should have. They stared out lifelessly from his bloated face. Mean black eyes above his tight bully's mouth. His arms were crossed on his chest, as if he'd been reading a book in bed and fallen asleep. There was a Bible on the floor beside him. I recognized the Bible. Just as I recognized the mark on his arm. The mark I'd been looking for since the day I'd first seen it in Lon Aamons's study. The snake's eye was ruby red; his coiled body the color of a fresh bruise. We'd found him, at last. We'd found Hack Lord.

Al walked over to the body and kneeled down beside it. "I wonder why he didn't shut the eyes," he said.

I stared at the Bible on the floor. I'd seen it that morning on a nightstand in the Lord house. Jake must have brought it with him from home. Perhaps that's the only reason he'd come all that way in the rain—to say a prayer over his poor,

222

misbegotten brother before the police found him in the morning. To say goodbye to his best friend.

"He's puffed up pretty good," Al said. "But you can see needle marks on his arm, all right. My guess is that he O.D.'d or just plain starved to death. Looks like he was in a bad way for a long time."

I looked at the dead man's face, at those lifeless black eyes and at the flesh surrounding them that had pouted like a piece of rotted fruit. It was almost as if he was looking at something on the opposite side of the room. On the wall, behind us.

"Give me your flashlight for a second, will you, Al?"

He handed it to me.

I flashed it along the wall beside the door. And there it was. The thing that Hack was still looking at, even in death. The same thing that had hung on Effie Reaves's wall in that nightmare trailer. A sketch of the Eden Park Overlook. The place where he'd killed Twyla Belton.

"Now what the hell does that mean?" Al said.

I stared at the picture and thought I knew, thought that I'd gotten a glimpse into that strange mind of his. It wasn't the beautiful park he'd cared about, it was the statue—the same one that Twyla had centered on. Only for him it had an entirely different meaning — that statue of two brothers suckled by a mother-wolf. For him, it was symbol of his own blighted family life and a key to what had caused him to go so terribly wrong. He'd left the same drawing in Effie's trailer—the same message. Because he'd had an artist's eye, after all, and the childhood trauma he'd never out-grown was his single theme. I was a little surprised that Jake had left it there for that long gaze of Hack's dead eye to see.

"Harry?" Al said suddenly. Something about his voice made me shiver and drop the flashlight beam to the floor.

I turned around and saw him kneeling again beside Hack. "When did you go out to that trailer park?" he said. "When was Effie Reaves killed?"

For a minute I couldn't think of it. So thoroughly had I tried to block that memory out of my mind. "Thursday. Thursday afternoon."

"We got a problem then," Al said in that unsettling tone of voice.

"What problem?"

He got to his feet and pulled a cigarette from his coat. His right hand was trembling a bit and that worried me more than the tremor in his voice. Something had shaken him up and he was not a man who was easily shaken. "Now I don't want to sound like George DeVries, but there is something fishy about this." He pointed to Hack's body. "I'm no forensic specialist, but I've seen my share of corpses. And, Harry, this one's been dead for a couple of days."

At first, it didn't sink in. "So, he's been dead for a couple of days, so what?"

"Yeah, but this is just Saturday morning," he said and glanced at his watch. "Two A.M., Saturday morning. And Effie was killed on Thursday afternoon around one."

I felt a thrill of terror run up my spine. "What are you saying, Al?"

"Well, Harry," he said almost bashfully. "I think all this time we might have been looking for the wrong man."

The S.W.A.T. team arrived at two-fifteen. They had a coroner in tow. The doctor—a silver-haired man with a cast in his right eye and the rumpled, ornery look of a country physician—spent about fifteen minutes examining Hack, then joined us out on the porch where we'd gathered to wait.

"I can't be sure of the exact time of death," he said casually. "Or of the cause. But he sure couldn't have murdered anyone on Thursday afternoon. Even if he wasn't dead, he wouldn't have had the strength to raise his arm."

"Jesus," I said out loud.

And then my mind went to work with a kind of blazing speed, running through alternatives, checking each one out; even though a part of me knew, without thinking, that there was only one real alternative that made sense of all I knew. There were those two boys on Ringold's list, Harry. The ones you never got around to checking. Only what did they have to do with Effie Reaves? And the answer was nothing. Well, there was Norris Reaves, then. Maybe he'd killed his sister over the speed, a business deal that had gone as bad as it could get. Only why would he cut her up that way—the way Twyla Belton and the library books had been cut up? He didn't know about the Belton girl or the books. So it couldn't have been Norris. And that left just the one. The one I didn't want to think about.

"Twyla Belton was killed two years ago," I said, putting it together once and for all.

Foster said, "Right."

"And when did Hack start living with Effie?"

He said it solemnly, as if he were fighting the same battle that I was. "Two years ago."

"And those damn books," I said. "Say he started tearing them up again a couple of months ago."

"Just about the time when Hack was really going to hell," Al said. "Really falling apart."

"Then Hack dies. Maybe in his arms. And he loses control. And instead of striking out randomly as he'd done two years before with Twyla, he kills the Reaves woman in a savage act of revenge."

"What the hell are you saying?" George DeVries said.

I walked into the house and upstairs to the back room. There was something I wanted to check out. Something crucial. As I stepped through the door, I heard Foster say it for me.

"We've been looking for the wrong brother, George. It was Jake doing the killing all along."

"Jake!" I heard him say. "That just isn't possible. What about that drawing? What about the tattoo? Twyla didn't implicate Jake."

Only she had, I thought, as I made my way up the dark stairs to the back of the house. Because he had been there, too. In the picture she'd drawn on that summery afternoon, two years before, in the Hyde Park Library. He had been there in the white background beyond his brother's tattooed arm. In the part of the page that was like an undeveloped print. Jake had been there, too. Jake was always there. Tag-along Jake. His big brother's shadow. He might even have watched her as she drew, seething inside because his brother had betrayed him by running away with a woman like his own despised mother. Then tearing up the books in the john, where Leo Sachs had seen him. Tearing them up, as if he were cutting up Hack himself—that paragon of talent and physical perfection. Tearing up, at one and the same time, the symbols of his brother and of the sexuality that he thought was destroying him. Jake, the good brother, the good son.

I walked into the room and stared again at Hack's dead eyes. But this time I tried to see the room from Jake's peculiar angle of vision. To see what he'd left behind him

226

to guide his pursuers. Because death itself was Jake's medium and this was a scene he had composed as carefully as he'd composed the one in Effie Reaves's trailer.

I looked into Hack's eyes and back at the wall at which he was staring. And I knew. "He's going to kill again," I said out loud.

Foster, who was standing in the doorway, said, "Maybe not. Maybe this is the end of it."

"Look for yourself, damn it!" I pointed to Hack's body and to the picture on the wall. "This has all been arranged, Al. Just like the crap in Effie's bedroom. He's got his brother staring at that damn statue again. It was just a yearbook picture of Hack in the trailer. But it's the same message—Haskell, the Overlook statue, and death. He's going to kill again tonight. We've got to get to a phone."

And then he understood, too. "Kate," he said and the cigarette fell right out of his mouth.

She was back at the Lord house at that very moment. Maybe searching his room.

25

I WOULDN'T want to repeat that drive back to Hyde Park—
racing through the dark and the rain to find . . . God only
knew what when we arrived. There isn't much that you
can't picture in your mind's eye. Your own death. The
death of a lover. But the image of Kate Davis torn to pieces
the way Effie Reaves had been torn apart . . . that was
something I didn't dare conjure up. That was something
that the saner part of me just wouldn't let me imagine. So
I didn't think at all. Just listened to the tires singing
through the rain and watched the rain-swept countryside
whirl past us in a blur, until the trees and hillsides died away
and we were coasting past storefronts and car lots and,

finally, past the sedate rows of yellow brick apartment houses and graceful colonials that marked the fringes of Hyde Park.

Al had radioed ahead, so there were cops all over Stettinius when we pulled up to the Lord house at about three-thirty. Blue lights were flashing from one end of the street to the other—like some seasonless celebration.

I didn't wait for Al to park. Just leaped out the side door as he pulled to the curb and ran through the rain up to the open door of the Lord home. A cop tried to block my way —a husky kid in a rain cap and slicker with his night stick dangling at his side. I shoved him aside so hard that he went down in the mud, then stepped over him and through the door. The mother was sitting on the stairs with her head in her hands and a weak look of pity on her face. When she saw me, she smiled grotesquely.

"They don't understand, Mr. Stoner," she said as if she'd been lost for hours and finally chanced upon someone who spoke her own language. "They've got it all confused. Jacob is a good boy, you know that. You tell them. Maybe, they'll believe you." She threw her hands up as if to say she'd tried herself, but they just wouldn't listen.

I walked up to her and wrenched her off the stairs. I must have been burning more adrenalin than I thought, because I actually picked her up off the ground, like a big straw doll. Her eyes got very large and she let out a yelp of terror.

"*You're* the one who doesn't understand!" I said through my teeth and shook her a little in rage.

I sat her back down on the stairs. Hard. She wrapped her arms around her breasts and held herself tightly. She was scared. I wanted her to be. I wanted something to get through that thick hide of hers.

"Your son Haskell is dead."

She nodded. "Dead."

"I know you don't care about that," I said almost hysterically. And for a second I wanted to club her so that she'd feel something outside of her own selfish circuit of emotions. But I held back. She was a lost cause anyway. And Kate still had to be found. So I played it the only way I knew would work. Her way.

I looked her in the eye and said, "If you don't want to see Jake dead, too, you'll tell me exactly what I want to know."

She nodded again.

"Because he's in great trouble."

She shook her head. "Not Jake."

"Yes, Jake!" I shouted at her.

She flinched. "He's not here. He left the house around midnight. Then he came back and went upstairs. When he found out what that friend of yours had done, he became very upset and left again."

"What do you mean? What did Kate do?"

"She took some of Jacob's pictures," Mrs. Lord said loftily. "I told her not to tamper with my boy's things. But she wouldn't listen. I wouldn't blame Jacob a bit for being upset with her."

"You wouldn't, huh?" I said and had to restrain myself from slapping her. "Did Kate say where she was going?"

Mrs. Lord blushed. "Why, to your apartment, Mr. Stoner. She was upstairs for quite a long time, looking through the boys' rooms. Then she came back down with two sketches and said she was going to your apartment. She seemed very excited. Frankly, I didn't understand her at all."

"When?" I said. "When did she leave?"

"At least an hour ago," the Lord woman said.

"And Jacob? When did he leave? "

"Around two-thirty, I think. Then all these people arrived . . ."

I whirled around on the stairs and ran back out the door. Al Foster was talking to a plainclothesman on the walk.

"She's at my place, Al," I shouted to him.

He nodded and said, "Let's go!"

It took us ten minutes more to get to the Delores—ten more minutes through the dark, slick streets of Hyde Park and east Walnut Hills. I didn't know what Kate had taken away with her when she left the Lord home—what it was that had made her so excited. All I knew was that Jacob hadn't liked it and that was enough to scare the hell out of me. When we hit Burnet Avenue at Melish, I turned on the car seat and tried to explain to the other men, as calmly as I could, what Mrs. Lord had told me. Then I gave them the lay-out of my apartment building, in case Jacob was waiting there.

"I live on the fourth floor of the Delores, toward the rear. Apartment E," I said. "There are two ways into the building. Through the lobby door and up the stairs or through the rear door at the head of the parking lot. Al and I will go in the front. George, you and Cal guard the back."

One of them said, "Fine."

I turned back to the dash and stared miserably at the raindrops beading up on the windshield. "If that crazy bastard has . . ." But I still couldn't think about it.

"It's going to be O.K., Harry," George DeVries said stoutly.

I kept repeating that—"It's going to be O.K. It's going to be O.K."—as we raced the last mile and a half down

231

Burnet to the Delores lot. When Al pulled over to the curb and stopped the engine, I turned back to DeVries and said, "Give me the shotgun."

He passed the short-barreled Winchester over the car seat, stock-end first. I opened the door, stepped out into the lot—the shotgun in my right hand—and gazed through the thin white mist of rain at the two rows of cars parked on the asphalt. The Pinto was there, all right, about halfway up the second row.

"At least she got this far safely," I said to Al.

He nodded. "Do you need a key to get in the lobby door?"

I shook my head. "But the rear one's locked." I pulled my house keys out of my pants pocket and tossed them over to Cal Levy. "It's the blue one, Cal. And the door's right over there." I pointed to a metal door set in the rear of the building between two rosebushes. "Give us a minute to get around to the front, then come on up."

Al and I walked quickly to the top of the lot, then up the four concrete steps, past the dogwoods, to the cement walkway that led to the lobby. I glanced up at my front window, but there was no light on inside. And that worried me. I pulled back the pump on the shotgun, flipped off the safety, and started to run. Once I got through the door, I bounded up the stairs two at a time, swinging around the banisters with one hand and clutching the shotgun with my other. By the time I got to the fourth floor landing, my thighs and lungs felt as if they were on fire.

I didn't wait for Al to catch up with me. Just marched straight down to my apartment and put my hand to the doorknob. The door opened effortlessly—it wasn't locked. I threw the shotgun to my shoulder and pointed the barrel into the room. Foster had made it upstairs by then. He was

232

leaning against the sash, his Police Special in his hand. I edged through the doorway into the darkness and whispered, "Kate?"

There wasn't a sound.

"I'm going to turn on a light, Al," I said.

I reached for the wall switch and flipped it on. For a second I had the eerie feeling I was in the wrong apartment. The lamp that usually stood by the couch was lying on the floor in front of the coffee table. In the dim, uneven light I could see the Zenith Globemaster sitting on its side like an unpacked box. Papers were scattered on the rug. And the baize armchair had been overturned and slashed open. White cotton stuffing dripped from the ripped cushion.

"Jesus," I whispered.

Then I started shouting—her name. Tearing through the apartment. Opening doors. Rifling closets. And shouting her name. But she wasn't there. At least, she wasn't there anymore.

"My God," I said helplessly to Foster. "He's got her!"

Al didn't say anything. I sat down on the couch and held my head in my hands. "Kate."

Levy and DeVries filed through the door and when they saw me sitting there, they looked away.

"What the hell could she have taken that would have made him come after her like this?" Foster said furiously. "What the hell was in those pictures?"

I stared at the papers scattered on the floor, but I couldn't make my voice work. My throat was too full of grief.

"If those pictures were what he was after," DeVries said, "why didn't he just take the damn things and . . . I mean he didn't do anything to the girl. At least, not in here."

He was right. There wasn't any blood on the floor. Or

any of the gruesome remains that the Ripper usually left behind him. In fact, once I'd made myself calm down, I realized that the room didn't look right at all—not, that is, if it had been the scene of a struggle. Nothing was broken. Not even the lamp that was lying in front of the coffee table. And Kate knew enough karate to have put up a fight that would have left half the room in shambles and awakened every tenant on the fourth floor. Jake had been in the apartment, all right. The slashed cushion told me that. But I began to think that Kate hadn't been there with him, that he must have tricked her into going back down to the lot or to the lobby, sapped her, then taken her keys and come up to the apartment on his own. But why would he have done that if, as George had said, the two drawings were all he'd been after? Perhaps he thought she'd hidden the pictures somewhere in the apartment. Only there wasn't any sign of a search. Just the pile of papers, the overturned lamp and radio, and the slashed-up chair.

There could only be one explanation for the look of the room, and the fact that I *wanted* to believe it—that I had to believe it, in order to keep from falling apart again—didn't make it any less reasonable. For some reason Jake Lord wanted me to know that he'd been in my apartment; he wanted me to know that he had taken Kate. Just as he'd wanted me to know that he was planning to kill again. Like the drawing he'd left in the farmhouse, the artful way he'd disarranged the room was meant to be another clue—something between a taunt and a cry for help, as if he were saying "this is what I'll do, if you don't stop me." I thought again of what Benson Howell had said about the games psychopaths played and knew that Jacob Lord was coming to the end of the match. He was declaring himself openly, serving his version of a final notice, challenging me to find him before he fulfilled his own prophecy and killed a third time.

But if it was a kind of game to him—a contest between pursuer and pursued—and if, as Howell had claimed, he actually wanted to be caught, then there had to be something else in that room that he'd left behind to guide me. If it was a game, he was waiting somewhere with Kate, waiting and watching to see if the hunter was shrewd enough for the prey. If I wasn't shrewd enough, if I didn't read his signals right . . . Kate would be dead. She could be dead at that moment, but I refused to believe it. I refused to believe that Jake would have gone to such trouble to abduct her, when, as DeVries had said, he could have killed her on the spot.

I stared at the papers scattered on the floor. Outside of the lamp, the radio, and the chair, they were the only anomalies in the room. Blank sheets of typing paper, mostly. A few bills that he could have pulled out of the rolltop desk. And something else. I got up from the couch and walked over to where they were lying on top of the pile. Two oversized sheets of drawing paper, torn from a sketch pad.

"What is that?" Foster said, as I picked one of them up.

I flipped it over and my heart began to pound in my chest. He *had* left something behind him to guide me. The drawing—probably one of the drawings that Kate had taken from his room—was another clue, another connection between what we'd found in the farmhouse and what was waiting for us somewhere in the night.

"What is it?" Foster said again.

I'd never seen her before. But I'd heard her described. Sweet, round face, like a child's drawing of mother. That's what Aamons had said. "I think it's a sketch of Twyla. Twyla Belton."

Al leaned over my shoulder and studied the drawing. "That's her, all right," he said grimly. "I saw her in the morgue when they brought her in."

Levy said, "Then he didn't take the drawings with him after all."

I bent down and picked up the second piece of paper, half-knowing, as I flipped it over, what would be on the other side. Knowing because it was the only thing that explained his actions, that explained why he'd taken Kate and why he let us know that he'd taken her.

"Good God!" Levy said as I held the picture at arm's length. "It's the girl!"

It was, indeed, a line sketch of Kate Davis — with the eyes and the mouth and the breasts and genitals neatly cut away. I dropped the sketch on the floor and sat down hard on the couch. I'd warned her it could happen when I'd first met her; but I hadn't really believed it. She hadn't believed it either. It had seemed so far-fetched, then. I could only imagine the thrill of terror she must have felt when she'd found her own likeness alongside the drawing of the dead girl, when she realized that it was she herself who was the Ripper's next intended victim. That was what had sent her rushing out of the Lord house and sent Jacob Lord after her.

It all made such terrifying sense. She'd started working at the library in late July, just about the time Hack had begun to fall apart and Jake had gone searching for his own kind of scapegoat. He must have watched her from the stacks, as she sat on that stool in front of the art shelves day after day, until the pretty blonde girl and the picture books and all the pain they stood for merged into a single obsession. He'd tried to resist it. Judging from what he'd left in my room, he was still trying. But it was a battle he wasn't

236

going to win. And that, I thought finally, was what he was trying to tell me, that was the real meaning of the slash mark and of the two pictures and of the drawing of the Overlook he'd left for his dead brother to see. He couldn't stop himself, unless someone got to him quickly.

But then Jake Lord had told me where he'd be. He'd told me twice. Once in the farmhouse. And once in my own living room, when he deliberately left the two pictures behind him—one of a girl he had murdered, one of a girl he was planning to kill.

"Let's go!" I said to the three men.

"Go where?" DeVries said.

"To where Jake said he'd be. To where he killed Twyla and where he'll kill again, if we don't stop him. To the Overlook in Eden Park."

26

It was almost five A.M. when we reached the circular drive of the Overlook on the northeast edge of Eden Park. Al pulled in beneath a clump of elder trees at the park gate. For a minute or two, we just stared up the road to where it curved beneath the low stone wall on top of the hillside. Lovers sat on that wall in the summertime and gazed down the hill at the riverlights and at the woody, moonlit hamlets on the Kentucky shore. In the afternoon or at twilight, it was a place for lovers. And for artists. The stone wall and the benches set beneath it and the small park in the middle of the circular drive, with its oak trees and its reflecting pool and its graceful walks and arched bridges and, of course, the statue—Jake's statue—gleaming in the soft, powdery light of a gas lamp. Somewhere in that beautiful little place, the Ripper was waiting like the serpent tatooed on his brother's arm. A serpent in a garden. Waiting to strike or to be trod under. I prayed we weren't too late.

"I'm going in alone," I said to Foster.

"The hell you are," he snapped.

"We don't have time to argue, Al. He's got Kate out there and he's been leaving a trail of breadcrumbs for me to follow since the first day he saw me. He *wants* me—maybe because I was the first one to put two and two together and come up with Twyla Belton. Who knows exactly how his mind works? But part of that madman in the park *wants* to be stopped. And I think I can reach that part. I think he thinks so, too. That's why he trashed the room when he didn't have to leave a clue. If he sees a whole army of us coming after him, he'll certainly kill her and maybe himself. I'm sure of it. That is, if he hasn't killed her already."

I cracked open the car door. "Stay out of it, Foster," I said. "The rest of you stay out, too. If you don't . . . when this thing is over, I'll kill you."

I slammed the door shut and walked quickly down the sidewalk and into Eden Park.

A gas light was sputtering beside a boarded-up refreshment stand on the east rim of the drive. I walked up to it, leaned against the siding, and waited. The Overlook wasn't a large park, but it was much too big for one man to cover. Anyway, I figured if I was right—if Jake really had been leaving clues for me to follow—then he'd come to me, once he was sure I was alone.

I stood by the slat shack for about five minutes, listening

to the rain dripping down the naked rock wall behind me and studying the tall oaks and the gaslit drive. Then I heard the footsteps. Even, unhurried footsteps, echoing above the patter of the rain. I put a hand to my brow and squinted through the drizzle until I saw him. He was stepping out of the shadows on the west side of the park. He was wearing a windbreaker and he had a green ski mask over his head.

I blew all the air I could out of my lungs, waited a second, then sucked in. The fresh oxygen made me a little giddy. I exhaled again, breathed in. Then I pulled the Colt Commander out of my shoulder holster, cocked it, flipped off the safety, and stuck it in my overcoat pocket. I took one more deep breath and walked out into the gaslight—to my rendezvous with Jacob Lord.

He'd seated himself on the low stone wall that runs around the crest of the hill. His hands were buried in his jacket pockets; his face was bent toward the sidewalk. He didn't look up when I sat down across from him on one of the benches. Just stared through the eyeholes in the ski mask at the rain-soaked pavement at his feet.

"Did you find Haskell?" he said after a moment.

"Yes."

"And the drawings?"

"Yes."

"I knew you would," he said and rolled his head a bit, side to side, like a little boy who's very pleased with himself. "You're a smart man—finding me out, like you did."

"I didn't do it alone, Jacob. I had some help."

"You mean your friend, Ms. Davis?"

I shook my head. "I mean you."

He looked up and I could see his teeth flash behind that mask. "I did give you a few hints, didn't I?"

"You did, indeed. Why do you think you did that, Jake?"

240

He shrugged. "Who can answer that question—why? Why did my brother have to die the way he did? Why am I like I am? Somebody probably knows, but he's not telling." Jacob put a finger to his lips and said, "I'm not telling, either. Do you want to know where Ms. Davis is?"

"Yes."

He laughed softly. "I thought you might. She's a very attractive woman. Don't you want to know what I've done to her?"

My hand clamped around the gun in my coat pocket. "What have you done to her?"

He shook his head. "I'm not going to tell you. Not yet. Not until I'm ready. And you know better than to try to force me." He crossed his legs and said, "Sometimes I think this is all Haskell's fault. I mean the way I am. He made it so easy. He was too tenderhearted. He let Mother push him around. Oh, God, the things I used to get away with when I was a kid. Stealing cookies, candy, money. She'd always blame him. It was always his fault. My poor, poor brother. Do you know how long it took the Reaves woman to die." Jacob snapped his fingers and rainwater shot from their tips. "But Hack . . . it took him two whole years. And he suffered every minute of every day. I was with him at the end. He made a true confession. I wouldn't feed him until he did. He'll be redeemed." Jacob gazed out into the night and said, "We'll all be redeemed."

"I can understand how you felt about Effie Reaves," I said. "But what about Twyla?"

"I don't know why I did that," he said remotely. "Do you always know why you do the things you do?"

I had to shake my head, no.

"Sometimes I'll just be sitting in my room reading. Only when I look down at the page, it's all torn up. Like I've been sketching, only I've cut things up." He looked down again at the sidewalk. "I cut them up. Like with my drawings, when I get mad because they're not right. You see, there's this gap between what's in here"—he tapped his forehead —"and . . ." He held up his hands and stared at them dispassionately. "It's as if they have a will of their own."

"And Kate," I said heavily. "Why her?"

"Something about the way she looked. Her hair, I think. That color of blonde, like coins on a tablecloth. Her body. There's something wrong with beauty—don't you know that? If it could stay inside, if it didn't touch the world, why then it would be fine. But it makes its way into your heart and then you burn. Can you take a live coal into your heart and not burn? That's what the Bible says. It says women turn men into crusts."

His eyes shifted behind the mask, but he didn't catch his mistake.

"Where is she now?" I asked him. "Where is Kate?"

"Oh, she's all right. I haven't killed her yet. She's down that hill on the right side of the park, tied to a tree. I told her I'd be back to finish when we were done. You know," he said as he pulled a long hunter's knife from his coat pocket, "you remind me of my brother. I can talk to you."

I stared at the knife in Jacob's hand and at the forlorn look in his eyes. "Don't!" I shouted. "Don't do it!"

Jake shook his head and whispered, "Too late."

He leaped off the stone wall, the knife cocked above his head, and I pulled the trigger of the Colt. It went off with a terrific bang, slamming my elbow into the back of the bench. The muzzle flash burned a hole through the coat pocket—a three foot tongue of fire that licked Jacob Lord's chest, lifted him off the pavement, and sent him flying backwards, in a bloody smear, all the way down the long, stony hillside to the river and to his death. The last look I saw in his eyes was one of almost gentle disappointment.

The gun blast was still echoing through the trees as I started running down the sidewalk to the west side of the park. It took me five minutes to find her in the dark, tied to an oak, halfway down the hill, a gag in her mouth. There was blood all over her blouse from where he'd been cutting her, and her face was sheet white. But when I fell to my knees beside her and cried, "Kate! Kate!" her eyelids flickered and I felt my heart move again inside my chest.

"You're going to be all right," I said fiercely and tore the gag from her mouth.

"It hurts," she whispered.

I untied her arms, lifted her off the ground, and carried her to the park road. Foster, Levy and DeVries were waiting at the top. I put her gently into the car and Al drove her to the emergency room at General.

27

KATE SPENT two days in Cincinnati General—getting sewn up and transfused and shot full of antibiotics and pain killers. I stayed beside her from morning to night. Every time I looked over at her, I saw her sassy, blonde face smiling up at me. It made me understand why hospitals didn't supply double beds.

"My hero," she'd say and bat her eyes.

It made me blush.

So did Miss Moselle, who showed up on Sunday evening with a ouija board and a bundle of papers under her arm. She sat down beside me and said, "I've finally finished your chart."

"And?" I said.

"You are a very unlucky man."

I laughed.

"But that will change in the next few months," she said with great assurance and smiled at Kate. "I see a long trip ahead of you. And romance."

"You do, huh?"

She reached into her purse and pulled out two plane tickets. "These are for you, Harry, darling," she said with real tenderness. "It was my idea, but Leon and the rest of the librarians chipped in. There's a check here, too, from Leon—for services rendered. He would have come by himself, but he was called downtown." Miss Moselle put a hand to her mouth and whispered, "I think he's finally going to be promoted. Things won't be the same without him," she said with a sigh.

"You'll break his replacement in quickly enough," I said.

She giggled.

I looked at the tickets, which were for Jamaica, and at the check, which was for twelve hundred and fifty dollars or one week's work, and said to Kate, "When are we going?"

Kate grinned and said, "We?"

"We."

"That suits me fine," she said. "You see I'm a changed woman. A completely reformed character."

"Completely?" I said.

She nodded and then she said, "Aren't I?"

We stopped at Potter's Field before we left. That's where the County had buried Jake Lord and his brother Haskell. Their mother had decided she wanted no part of the funeral. It was a cold blue day with a wafer of a moon in the eastern sky and just a trickle of wind running down the grassy hillside. There wasn't any headstone, just a mound of fresh earth. We had to ask the digger—a seedy-looking hillbilly with a red bandana around his head—which graves they were buried in.

He looked at a placard hanging on his tool shed and said, "They're buried together. One atop t'other." Then he coughed and said, "Saves space. Couple others buried with 'em."

He showed us to the grave and I stood there for a minute looking at the freshly turned earth.

"I still feel sorry for them," Kate said. "In spite of . . . of everything. Don't you?"

"I don't know," I said. "He doesn't seem real to me. I guess he never will. You know I must have talked to a dozen people last week, some of them pretty knowledgeable folks, and I still don't understand Jake Lord."

"Let's go," Kate said with a shiver.

I took her hand and we walked back up the dirt path to the car. A little boy, probably the gravedigger's son, was sitting on the ground, playing mumblety-peg with a pen-knife. I watched him through the rearview mirror as we drove off and thought of Jake Lord. Then Kate tugged at my arm and smiled at me. And all I wanted to think about was her.